GARDEN OF SECOND CHANCES

C. DEANNE ROWE

CITRINE GROUP, LLC

Garden Of Second Chances

Published by C. Deanne Rowe

www.cdeannerowe.com

Cover Art by Rebecca K. Sterling

Created with Vellum

Garden Of Second Chances is dedicated to the women in my life who I know I can turn to if I am in need.

1

SEEDS OF HOPE

Emily Hawthorne stepped cautiously into the overgrown garden, her auburn hair catching the last rays of the sun as her boots sank into the soft, untamed earth. Dressed in her usual earth-toned blouse and jeans, she looked ready to engage with the land—a stark contrast to the polished attire she'd worn in the city.

The cool air carried the familiar scents of damp soil and wild herbs mingling with the subtle sweetness of honeysuckle. She reached out, brushing a hand across the tangled vines. The leaves beneath her fingers seemed to shimmer faintly, their emerald edges catching the fading sunlight in a way that felt too deliberate to be natural. A soft breeze, carrying a fleeting whisper of laughter and a the fleeting scent of roses that wasn't there a moment before. A tangle of memories surfaced, vivid as the wildflowers pushing up through the weeds. Her grandmother, Cora, had once guided her small hands over these very plants, pointing out which needed care and which could be left to grow on their own.

The sun slipped lower, casting the mountains in a hazy blue hue. Emily paused on a thorny branch, feeling it prickle against her skin, and exhaled, absorbing the garden's silent welcome. She dug her fingers into the soil, tightening her grip as she remembered her grandmother's whispered stories of fairies and hidden magic. It all felt distant, yet close enough to touch.

Her mind wandered back to the magical summers of her youth spent under her grandmother's loving care. The days when the world was brimming with possibilities, and the air itself seemed infused with wonder. Her grandmother would lead her through the garden, her voice a soft melody as she spoke of the garden fairies and the enchantment that filled every corner of the land. "These fairies," Cora would say, her eyes twinkling with mischief, "they protect our garden and help it grow. You just have to believe, my dear."

Emily smiled, a bittersweet feeling rising in her chest as she recalled those carefree days. She would spend hours searching for the elusive fairies, convinced she saw a flicker of wings or heard their tiny laughter. The garden had been a world of magic and joy, where her childish heart was free to dream and imagine, and her grandmother's stories painted her life with vibrant hues of fantasy and hope. But as she grew older, that magic slowly faded into the background, overshadowed by the demands of adulthood and the practicalities her mother so often imposed.

Claire Martin Wren was a practical woman who believed in hard facts and tangible results. She often scolded Emily for what she termed "living in a fantasy world," trying to steer her daughter away from what she considered childish nonsense. Over time, Emily's visits to the farmhouse became fewer, and the vivid colors of her childhood dreams dulled into the sepia tones of memories.

Her thoughts drifted to a conversation she had with her mother just a few months ago, a memory she couldn't seem to shake. Emily rubbed her temples, noticing the familiar tension build as she recalled her mother's words. She was sitting in her living room, surrounded by the noise of the bustling streets outside. She had just ended a tense conversation with Mark about their latest failed attempt at IVF, feeling lost, suffocated by the walls of her own home. On impulse, she picked up the phone and called her mother, seeking solace or perhaps understanding.

After their normal exchange, Emily asked, "Mom, do you remember grandmother's garden? How she used to talk about the fairies and all that magic?"

The line was quiet for a moment before her mother's sigh cut through. "Those were just stories," Claire said, her tone softening. "Your grandmother had a way with tales, but they were for children."

Emily's jaw tightened. "They felt real to me. I need that... I need something that feels right again." Her voice faltered, but she kept going. "That's why I want to go back to the farmhouse for a while."

"Back there?" Her mother's disbelief was audible, almost sharp. "You have a life here. A career. What do you expect to find in that empty house?"

Emily had looked out the window, her grip tightening on the phone. "Maybe a part of myself," she replied softly. "I've lost something here, Mom, and I think it's there."

Another silence. She could almost see her mother, lips pressed together, a frown creasing her brow. "Life isn't about running off to chase fantasies, Emily. You're not a child."

The words stung, but Emily took a steady breath. "Maybe that's exactly the problem. Maybe I need to believe in something again."

This time, her mother didn't respond. When the silence grew heavy, Emily ended the call herself, feeling the tension dissolve, replaced by a quiet, unfamiliar determination.

As the memory faded, she blinked and refocused on the present, her gaze falling upon the quiet of the garden. Inheriting her grandmother's old farmhouse, an unexpected bequest from a past that seemed both distant and deeply ingrained, offered a temporary refuge. But more than that, it provided a chance for Emily to reconnect with the joy and magic she remembered from her youth. She hadn't come to Blue Ridge Haven just to escape her pain. She rediscovered the part of herself that still believed in magic, in the possibilities that once seemed so endless.

In the farmhouse's solitude, surrounded by the untamed beauty of the land, Emily understood that this separation was not just necessary but transformative. It was a chance to rediscover herself outside the identity of a woman grappling with infertility and a failing marriage, to find solace in the land her grandmother had once tended with love and care. Standing there, the weight of the years pressing in on her, Emily felt a surge of determination. Her hands, though unused to the rigors of gardening, were ready to dig into the earth, to reconnect with a legacy that had lain dormant for too long.

The garden was not just a forgotten plot of land. It was a bridge to her past, to the joy and magic she had lost along the way and was desperate to regain. The vibrant arts scene, the community's warm embrace, and the breathtaking beauty of the mountains that cradled Blue Ridge Haven seemed a world away from this neglected spot. Yet, as Emily stood there, a figure of resilience framed against the backdrop of decay and potential rebirth, she embodied the very essence of Blue Ridge Haven—a place steeped in mystery and ancient magic.

The decision to stay and restore the garden didn't come as an epiphany but as a quiet realization that perhaps healing could be found nurturing life from the soil. The town of Blue Ridge Haven seemed to call to her, a reminder of the world just beyond the shadows of the past. Tomorrow, she would begin the work of clearing away the weeds, of breathing life back into the garden—and into herself. It was a daunting task, but in a community where art and nature danced in harmonious balance, Emily sensed the stirrings of a second chance. A return to the magic she once believed in and to the joy that could give her a reason to embrace life again. The distance from her sorrow would allow her to see their struggles from a new perspective. There was hope in the possibility of new beginnings, not just for the garden, but for her own life, with or without Mark.

Wandering through the quiet farmhouse, her gaze fell upon the walls adorned with photographs of flowers she had taken during her stays at the farmhouse—a silent testament to her grandmother Cora's love for the garden and its myriad blooms. One particular photo caught her eye—a delicate iris, her favorite flower, captured in the golden light of dawn. It was more than just a photo. It was a memory, a piece of her childhood wrapped in the warm hues of summer mornings spent in the garden, searching for fairies and listening to her grandmother's stories.

With a gentle touch, Emily took the framed photo off the wall, her fingers tracing the edges as if to unearth the stories it held. As she flipped it over, a letter slipped out from behind the frame, its edges worn with time. It was addressed to her in her grandmother's handwriting. Her heart quickened as she unfolded the paper, Cora's words flowing like a whisper through time.

My dearest Emily,

I always knew you'd be drawn to the iris—it's as resilient and beautiful as you are. If you're reading this, it means you've found your way back to the place that holds our family's heart. The garden knows no season, only neglect. It's now in your hands, my dear, to breathe new life into it, to nurture it back to its former glory.

This garden is not just a plot of land. It's a legacy of love, patience, and perseverance. I leave it to you, not as a burden, but as a gift—a chance to find healing, to rediscover yourself amid the beauty of nature. Let it be your canvas, Emily. Plant new seeds, tend to them with care, and watch as new life takes root, both in the garden and within you. There is magic here, ancient and powerful. It was the power to heal, to renew. Trust in it and in yourself.

With all my love,

Grandmother Cora

Tears blurred Emily's vision as she finished reading. The letter was a relief. A guiding light from her grandmother, urging her to embrace the garden's potential for renewal. Clutching the letter close, she knew what she needed to do. Tomorrow, she would begin reclaiming the garden, armed with Cora's wisdom and the promise of new beginnings. The garden was more than a project. It was a path to healing, a second chance at life's unfurling beauty.

The act of clearing the garden, pulling weeds, and planting new life could become a metaphor for her own healing—a reclamation of lost hope and renewal of spirit. With each new bloom that fought its way through the soil, Emily hoped to find pieces of herself she'd thought were lost forever. As she thought back to her childhood, she remembered more of her grandmother's stories, the whispered secrets of the garden fairies, and the magic that once was so real. The garden, like her, was in a state of becoming, transforming under the gentle care of patience and perseverance.

Her mother might still dismiss these old tales as childish fantasies, but Emily had an unshakable bond to the magic of the garden—a legacy that was as real and rooted as the ancient trees around her.

2

WHISPERS OF THE NIGHT

The sun dipped below the peaks of the Blue Ridge Mountains as Emily finished exploring the farmhouse. The day had been a whirlwind of emotions—bittersweet memories colliding with the reality of her present struggles. Now, as night fell, the house seemed both comforting and eerie, filled with the echoes of a past that seemed to linger in every corner.

The creaking of the wooden stairs under her feet was a familiar sound, one that pulled her back to the carefree summers she had spent with her grandmother Cora. Those were the days when the world was simple and full of wonder when the garden outside had been a place of magic and endless possibility. Every corner of the house, every rustle of the leaves outside, had seemed alive with the promise of adventure and the enchantment of her grandmother's stories.

Emily spent the first night in the bedroom that had always been hers during those summers. It was a small, cozy room at the end of the hall, with floral wallpaper that had faded over the years and a quilt on the bed that her grandmother had made by hand. The sight of it brought a soft smile to her lips, a sense of comfort she hadn't felt in a long time. It was as if the room itself remembered her and was welcoming her back with open arms.

She pushed the door open wider and stepped inside, setting her suitcase down on the floor. The room smelled faintly of lavender and old wood, a scent that was both calming and nostalgic. As she unpacked, carefully placing her clothes in the antique dresser, her eyes caught something unexpected—a small, familiar shape resting against the pillows on the bed.

Emily paused, her heart skipping a beat as she recognized the doll. It was Rosie, her childhood companion, made from soft, worn fabric and bright button eyes. The doll sat propped up as if waiting for her, the same way she had all those years ago.

A wave of emotions washed over her as she picked up Rosie, her fingers tracing the familiar stitching. Memories came flooding back—nights spent in this very bed, clutching Rosie close, feeling safe and protected. Even as she grew older and her visits to the farmhouse became less frequent, she never forgot the comfort Rosie brought her. But as life grew more complicated and the magic of childhood faded, Rosie was left behind, a relic of simpler times.

Emily hugged the doll to her chest, closing her eyes. How had it ended up on the bed waiting for her? Emily couldn't remember the last time she saw it, and yet here it was, as if it had been expecting her return. Did someone find it and place it here, or...was it something else? A shiver ran down her spine—not of fear, but of something deeper, something that seemed like a connection to the past, to the magic her grandmother had always believed in. It was as though Rosie had been waiting for Emily to come back, to help remind her of the joy and wonder she had once known.

With Rosie in her arms, she sat on the edge of the bed, letting the memories wash over her. She had been so consumed by sorrow for what she couldn't have—by the pain of infertility and the growing distance from Mark—that she had forgotten the joy of what she had. This place, this garden, and the legacy her grandmother had left her. She thought back to the long nights spent with Mark, the empty crib they had never used, and the unspoken grief that seemed to fill every room of their house. Perhaps the magic was still here, a quiet, enduring kind rooted in love and patience.

A tear slipped down Emily's cheek as she held the doll close to her chest. It felt like reconnecting with a part of herself she thought she had lost. She knew that tomorrow, she would begin restoring the garden, breathing new life into the land her grandmother had cherished. But tonight, she would take comfort in the presence of Rosie, just as she had when she was a child.

With a newfound sense of peace, Emily placed Rosie back on the pillow, then continued unpacking her suitcase. She found her nightgown and decided she would finish the rest tomorrow. Her old bed was calling her name. As she slid under the quilt, she kept the doll close, just like she used to, and closed her eyes. The house creaked softly around her. The wind whispered through the trees outside, but she felt safe, protected by the gentle magic that had always been a part of this place.

That night, as she drifted into sleep, her dreams were filled with images of the garden as it once was—vibrant and full of life, flowers blooming in every corner, the air thick with the scent of jasmine and lavender. And during it all, she saw her grandmother smiling at her with eyes full of love and pride.

"Trust in the magic," her grandmother's voice echoed softly through her dreams. "And trust in yourself."

Emily stirred slightly in her sleep, a peaceful smile on her lips. The garden, the house, and Rosie—everything was coming together, weaving a tapestry of memories and new beginnings. And as the moonlight streamed through the window, Rosie watched over her, ensuring that her dreams were sweet and her heart was light.

Outside, a gentle breeze rustled the leaves of the old oak tree, and for a moment, Emily could have sworn she heard a soft whisper—a quiet murmur that seemed to carry the promise of the garden's revival and, perhaps, the revival of her own spirit.

3

THE SEEDS OF A NEW BEGINNING

The morning sun glowed over the old farmhouse as Emily stood on the porch, surveying the overgrowth. It was almost two acres of a wild tapestry of green, with hints of color from resilient flowers that had thrived despite the neglect. She took a deep breath, the scent of earth filling her lungs, a mix of daunting challenge and undeniable allure. As the first light touched the leaves, a faint shimmer sparkled across the garden, hinting at the magic hidden within.

A pang of nostalgia hit her as she gazed about, remembering how, as a child, she had seen this very place as a world of endless possibilities. Back then, every flower, every stone seemed to hold a secret, whispered to her by the wind and carried on the wings of butterflies. The garden had been her sanctuary, a place where her grandmother's stories of fairies and magical blooms made the world seem alive with wonder. Now, she was determined to reclaim that joy, to bring back the magic that once made this a place of dreams.

She had just outlined her plans for the day, determined to make a start on the restoration process, when her phone rang, slicing through the morning's calm. Glancing at the caller ID, she saw her mother's name flashing on the screen. She hesitated a moment before answering.

"Hi, Mom," she greeted her with a slight apprehension.

"Emily, darling, how are you?" Claire's voice came through, carrying that familiar tone of concern and curiosity.

"I'm fine," Emily said, her tone calm.

"Mark told me you're in Blue Ridge Haven. What in heaven's name are you doing there?" Claire asked.

"I came to check on the farmhouse. And while I'm here, I've decided to restore the garden, to bring it back to life, just like Grandma Cora would have wanted," Emily responded, her voice steady but with an underlying current of emotion.

"Emily, you need to be practical," Claire insisted, her voice edged with frustration. "I thought we'd already had this discussion. You're hiding out there, clinging to this garden like it's going to solve all your problems. That's not how life works."

Emily's grip tightened on the phone. The sting of her mother's words landed like a blow. "It's not just a garden, Mom," she replied, her voice trembling with anger and pain. "It's my chance to find some peace, to reconnect with who I was before...before everything fell apart."

Claire's silence was heavy, and when she finally spoke, her tone was sharp, almost brittle. "Before what? Before your marriage hit a rough patch. Before you ran away?" Her words cut through the distance like a knife. "You can't just retreat into your fantasies whenever life gets hard."

Emily's heart pounded in her chest. She swallowed, her throat tight. "I'm not running away," she said, struggling to keep her voice steady. "I'm trying to find something real, something that matters to me. Why can't you understand that?"

For a moment, the only sound was the faint static on the line. Then Claire sighed, a sound filled with years of unresolved tension. "I don't want you to end up like her."

"Like who?" Emily asked, her voice barely a whisper, though she already knew the answer.

"Like your grandmother," Claire whispered. "Chasing dreams and stories instead of facing reality."

Emily's breath hitched. A tear slipped down her cheek. "Mom, you know how much I love teaching, right? Helping others find their voice through writing, it's rewarding..." Her voice faltered, and she took a deep breath, steadying herself. "But the truth is, I've been feeling lost, Mom. The infertility struggles... they've been harder on me than I've let on. Mark and I... well, you know that story." She paused, her voice breaking. "I need a break, a change of scenery, something to help me heal and find a piece of myself again."

There was a moment of silence on the line, and when Claire spoke again, her voice was softer, more hesitant. "I don't understand how playing in the dirt will help you heal."

Emily continued, the words flowing more freely now. "Mom, it's not just about fixing up an old patch of land. It's about reconnecting with something deeper. Something Grandmother and I shared. I'm just going through the motions every day. I've taken a leave of absence from teaching to find some healing here. I need more."

She paced the edge of the overgrown garden, her boots sinking slightly into the damp, thawing earth. The air was crisp and carried the faint, fresh scent of new growth mingling with the last traces of winter. Budding shoots peeked tentatively through the tangle of weeds, and here and there, a stray vine stretched toward the pale sunlight as if the garden itself was stirring awake, reluctant to remember the weight of neglect.

Claire's voice softened further, the worry still there but mixed with a hint of understanding. "Emily, darling, I may not fully understand this...this passion for the garden. But I understand the need to find yourself again. Just promise me, don't let your head stay in the clouds like your grandmother's. I want you to find peace, but I also want you to be okay."

A surge of gratitude filled her, tears pricking her eyes. "Thanks, Mom. That means more than you know. Maybe through this garden, I can rebuild, find some peace and understand where I belong."

Their call ended with promises to keep in touch, leaving Emily standing on the porch, her heart heavy yet lighter at the same time, a blend of apprehension and hope stirring within her. Her mother's words, though hesitant, offered a semblance of support she hadn't realized she needed. Now, more than ever, she knew the garden was where she needed to be—a place where new beginnings might just take root and where the magic she once believed in could be found again.

Emily ended the call and stood in silence for a moment, letting the conversation settle. She looked out over the garden, its wild beauty calling her, a symbol of the life she was trying to reclaim. She wiped a tear from her cheek. A strange mix of relief and resolve rushed through her. She knew her mother didn't fully understand, but that was okay. This journey was hers alone to make.

She stared at her phone for a moment longer, her mother's words echoing in her mind: *Don't let your head stay in the clouds like your grandmother's.* She set the phone down and walked to the edge of the porch, her eyes drifting to the garden. A pang of longing for the comfort of her grandmother's presence hit her, the way Cora's stories had always made the world seem alive with magic. She closed her eyes, and a memory washed over her, transporting her back to a simpler time.

Eight-year-old Emily sat on the porch steps beside her grandmother. The twilight sky was painted in hues of orange and pink, the first stars just beginning to twinkle. The garden stretched out before them, bathed in the soft, fading light of the day.

"See those lights?" Cora whispered, her voice warm and gentle. "Those are the fairies watching over the garden. They help everything grow."

Young Emily's eyes widened with wonder as she squinted into the twilight, trying to see the tiny, glowing lights her grandmother spoke of. "Really? Can I see them up close?" She leaned forward, her small hands gripping the edge of the step in anticipation.

Before Cora could answer, Claire appeared in the doorway behind them. She looked tired, a deep crease etched between her brows. "Cora, please." Her voice was weary, edged with frustration.

"Can we not fill her head with all this nonsense? She needs to focus on things that are real, things that matter."

Emily turned, her face falling slightly at the interruption. Cora, however, merely smiled, a twinkle in her eyes as she looked up at her daughter-in-law. "Oh, Claire, let her dream a little. There's nothing wrong with a bit of magic in the world."

"She doesn't need magic." Claire's voice was firm, her expression stern. "She needs to learn how to live in the real world."

The words hung in the air, heavy and final. Emily looked from her mother to her grandmother, sensing a tug in her heart, torn between the practical world her mother spoke of and the magical one her grandmother believed in. A pang of sadness settled in her chest, a sense of something slipping away, something precious.

"The real world isn't always so black and white, Claire," Cora said softly, turning her gaze back to Emily. "Sometimes, it's the things we can't see that matter the most."

Claire shook her head. She turned to go back inside, but not before giving Cora one last look. "Don't fill her head with things that aren't real. She needs to be prepared for what's out there, not what's in here." She gestured vaguely at the garden, then turned and disappeared into the farmhouse.

Emily watched her mother go, having a mix of emotions she couldn't quite name. She looked up at her grandmother, who was still smiling, her eyes filled with understanding.

"Don't worry about your mother," she whispered, wrapping an arm around Emily's shoulders. "She just wants what's best for you in her own way. But remember, there's room for magic too."

Emily nodded, leaning into her grandmother's embrace, her eyes drifting back to the garden. She could have sworn she saw a tiny light flicker among the leaves, a little spark of hope in the growing darkness.

She blinked, the memory fading like the last light of the day. She looked out at the garden, noticing the familiar pull of her grandmother's words, the belief in something more. Her mother's practicality was always a shadow over her dreams, but here, she could still feel the magic. She still believed.

The sound of the gate creaking open drew her attention to the figure of Margaret Ellis, known to all, especially Emily, as Maggie, making her way up the path. Maggie's presence was like a gentle breeze, bringing a sense of calm and certainty. Her silver hair shone in the sunlight, and her eyes sparkled with an energy that opposed her years. She was the same age as Grandmother Cora and a steadfast friend. Maggie was a light in the darkness of grief when Emily needed her most.

"Good morning, Emily," Maggie greeted her with a warm smile, her voice smooth and soothing, like a favorite melody. "Looks like you're trying to make sense of things," she said, her eyes taking in the wild expanse with a knowing glance.

Emily returned the smile, relieved at the sight of her. "Good morning, Maggie. I was just trying to figure out where to start. It appears the garden is a bit of a lost cause."

Maggie chuckled softly as she reached Emily. "Oh, my dear, this isn't a lost cause. This is a canvas waiting for new life to be painted upon it. Your grandmother's spirit still dances here, in every leaf, every petal. It just needs someone to coax it back to life, to remind it what it's capable of."

Emily noticed small, twinkling lights flitting among the flowers—tiny ethereal beings she hadn't noticed before as they walked together into the heart of the garden. Maggie saw the surprise on her face and smiled, a twinkle in her own eyes.

"Ah, I see you've spotted the garden fairies," Maggie whispered. "They're shy but incredibly helpful. They've watched over this garden for generations, assisting those who tend to it with a pure heart."

Emily watched in awe as one fairy landed on a nearby flower, its wings shimmering in the sunlight. "I remember now," she whispered. "It's like this place is alive in ways I'd forgotten."

Maggie nodded. "Oh, it's very much alive. Your grandmother knew how to listen to the land, to work with its magic. You've got the same gift. It's in your blood. The garden has been in mourning for your grandmother. Waiting for the next caretaker to come along."

At Maggie's words, a vivid memory surfaced in Emily's mind. She was a little girl, her small hand clasped in Grandmother Cora's weathered one, walking along the same path. The sun was setting, casting a warm glow over the flowers, and young Emily's eyes widened with wonder as she saw a tiny light dancing among the petals.

"Grandmother, look! Fireflies!" Emily had exclaimed.

Grandmother Cora had smiled, her eyes twinkling with a secret only she knew. "Those aren't fireflies, my sweet. Those are garden fairies. They help the plants grow and keep the garden healthy."

"Fairies?" Emily's voice was filled with awe.

"Yes, dear. They're shy but kind. If you care for the garden with love, they'll always be here to help you," Cora had said, her voice gentle and full of wisdom. She had knelt down, bringing Emily to her level. "This garden is special. It's alive with magic. Always remember to treat it with respect and love, and it will flourish."

The memory faded, and a renewed sense of purpose engulfed Emily. The garden was more than a project. It was a legacy, a living testament to her grandmother's love and the magic she always believed in.

Maggie pointed out various plants and their conditions, her voice a soothing stream of knowledge and encouragement. "This is a peony bush, a resilient soul that blooms despite the odds. And over there, see the rosemary? It's a symbol of remembrance, fitting for your grandmother's garden," she explained, her words painting the picture of what the garden could become.

Emily listened, captivated by Maggie's vision. The daunting task ahead seemed more like an adventure, a chance to connect with her grandmother's legacy and create something beautiful.

"Would you help me restore it?" Emily asked, a hopeful note in her voice. "I want to bring this garden back to life, to make it a place of beauty and memory, but I don't know if I can do it alone and my mother believes I'm wasting time that could be better used focusing on my career."

Maggie placed a gentle hand on Emily's shoulder, her gaze kind and reassuring. "Oh, Emily, you won't have to do it alone. I'll be right here with you every step of the way. Together, we'll breathe new life into this garden, and who knows? You might just find some new growth within yourself as well."

Their shared laughter mingled with the sounds of the garden, a promise of the journey ahead. As they made plans, the plants and flowers seemed to listen, the surrounding wildness tinged with the promise of renewal and the bond of a beautiful friendship. The fairies danced in the light, and the ancient magic of the garden stirred, ready to awaken under their care.

4

A NEW HAND IN THE GARDEN

The last echoes of their laughter faded, and the serene morning gave way to the bustling energy of a new day. With its overgrowth and hidden treasures, the garden seemed to watch in delicate expectation as Maggie and Emily laid plans for its revival. Their shared vision—a blend of beauty, memory, and the spirit of Emily's grandmother—was a bond that drew them closer, a project that promised not just the restoration of the land but of their own spirits.

The sound of gravel under tires signaled an arrival as they outlined their first steps. Maggie glanced at her watch, a look of realization dawning on her face. "Ah, that will be Alex. I'd almost forgotten he's due to fix the kitchen window today."

Emily, curiosity piqued, followed Maggie to greet the newcomer. Alex Bennett, with his amiable smile and toolbox in hand, was a stark contrast to the garden's wildness. His presence brought an extra element to the day, a reminder of the world beyond the garden's confines.

Maggie introduced them, mentioning Alex's knack for fixing things, a talent that seemed even more valuable amid the garden's needed care.

He appeared to be in his late thirties, around six feet tall, with a rugged charm Emily could only guess came from years of physical work. His short, sandy-brown hair looked tousled as if he ran his hands through it a few times too many. His striking green eyes were observant and kind, reflecting a depth of character and an innate warmth. His clothing seemed practical workwear: sturdy boots, denim jeans, and a flannel shirt that seemed to add to his approachable demeanor.

He was quick to offer his help, not just with the window but with the garden as well. "I've been known to have a green thumb when the occasion calls for it," he said with a grin, his eyes crinkling at the corners. "I grew up working in my mother's garden. She always said that tending to plants was a lot like peopling—you have to be patient, give them room to grow."

Emily chuckled. "Well, I'm glad to know you have some experience. This place could use a little patience, that's for sure."

Alex nodded thoughtfully, glancing around at the overgrown landscape. "Places like this are worth the effort. Besides, I could use a break from fixing windows and fences. Working with the earth sounds more...grounding." He cast a sideways glance at Maggie and then back to Emily. "And I figure if I help here, I might get some of Maggie's famous apple pie in return."

Maggie laughed, a light sound that brightened the air. "You know the way to my heart, Alex. You help us turn this jungle back into a garden, and I'll bake you the best pie you've ever tasted."

His offer and the easy camaraderie he already shared with Maggie surprised Emily. "I'll keep you in mind," she replied, getting a spark of hope.

By the time the window latch clicked back into place, a new understanding had taken root among them. The garden's revival was no longer just a project for Maggie and Emily but a community endeavor, a collective step toward renewal.

Alex packed up his tools, promising to return with ideas and perhaps some seedlings. Maggie and Emily stood at the doorway, watching him drive away. The garden, once a symbol of daunting challenge, now represented a future filled with growth for plants and blooming friendships.

"Looks like our garden project just got bigger," Maggie said, a smile in her voice.

Emily nodded, her heart light with anticipation. "And so has our circle. It's funny how life works, isn't it? Just when you think you're focusing on bringing new life to a garden, you end up nurturing so much more."

Maggie gave her a knowing look. "You've always had a way of drawing people in, just like your grandmother."

Emily smiled softly, touched by the older woman's words. "I hope so."

They turned back to the garden, its wildness now a canvas of possibility, a shared dream just beginning to sprout. Together, with Alex's unexpected contribution, they were ready to embark on a journey of transformation—a journey that promised to bring beauty not only to the garden but to their lives as well.

While they mapped out their next steps, a lone figure approached from the path that wound through the mountain landscape. A tall and slender man with hair the color of autumn leaves and eyes that seemed to reflect the changing seasons. His presence was almost otherworldly.

"Maggie, good morning!" he called out as he approached, his voice carrying a melodic resonance that seemed to blend with the natural sounds around him. His gaze swept over the lush, chaotic growth with a look of keen interest, his eyes glinting like emeralds in the sunlight.

"Liam, perfect timing," Maggie exclaimed. "We could really use your expertise right now." She turned to Emily and said, "Liam Wilder is known in Blue Ridge Haven for his deep connection to the natural world."

An aura of mystique surrounded the man. Emily smiled warmly, extending her hand in greeting. "Liam, I'm so glad to meet you."

Liam took her hand gently, his touch warm despite the cool

morning air. "The pleasure is mine, Emily. I've heard a lot about you —mostly from the garden," he added with a teasing smile.

Emily laughed, intrigued. "Oh really? And what has the garden been saying?"

Liam's expression grew more serious, his eyes taking on a thoughtful look. "It's been waiting for someone like you—a caretaker who understands its magic, someone who's willing to listen."

Spending more time with the man and seeing his connection to Maggie, Emily realized the addition of Liam to their small team was more than just practical. It was inspirational. His knowledge of botanical lore and understanding of the mystical connections between plants and people promised to deepen the restoration project in ways she had only hoped for. Together, they wove new dreams for the old garden, each bringing their own strengths to the revitalization effort, bound by a shared love for the land and a commitment to see it flourish.

They walked between plants and trees and discussed plans and possibilities. The surrounding air seemed charged with potential. The garden was awakening, and with Liam's arrival, it seemed poised to reclaim its former glory and perhaps reveal a few of its hidden wonders.

They discussed their plans as a soft, melodic humming filled the air, drawing their attention to a cluster of flowers glowing with a gentle, ethereal light. At times, Liam would pause, tilting his head as though he was hearing something inaudible.

"Those are the Luminaria blossoms," Liam explained with a smile, guiding Emily to the plant that appeared to be blooming. "They only bloom when the garden senses true caretakers. It's a sign that the garden's magic is awakening."

Emily watched in awe as the flowers swayed, their light illuminating the surrounding foliage. "It's beautiful. I did not know the garden held such wonders."

Liam nodded. His gaze was distant, as if seeing beyond the physical realm. "This garden is special, Emily. It's connected to the ancient magic of the land. It will reveal more of its secrets as we nurture it and aid us in our journey."

Her heart swelled with a sense of belonging, the sense that she was exactly where she needed to be. "Thank you, Liam," she said softly, "for helping us see the magic."

With a renewed sense of purpose, Emily, Maggie, and Liam continued to map out their next steps, knowing that their efforts were not just about restoring a garden but about uncovering the magical legacy left by Cora Wren. Their connection grew with each new discovery. Not only to the garden but to each other, forming bonds that would carry them through the challenges ahead.

As they turned back to the house, a soft breeze rustled the leaves overhead, and Emily had a sudden warmth at her back, like a gentle hand guiding her forward. She paused for a moment, glancing over her shoulder, but saw nothing out of the ordinary. Just the garden, bathed in the golden light of the afternoon.

But something in the air had changed—a subtle shift, a whisper of magic that seemed to linger, promising that the garden's secrets were only just beginning to unfold. A quiet thrill ran through her. She suspected that the days ahead would be filled with surprises.

5

NEW GROWTH

Kneeling in the dirt, Emily cradled the tender life of a seedling. Maggie, Liam, and Alex each grabbed a tool and settled in beside her. As they worked, the garden, once a symbol of neglect, was transforming into a place of healing and hope under their combined efforts. The earth beneath their fingers appeared alive, responding to their touch as if recognizing the care they were pouring into it. It pulsed faintly with light for a moment, as though acknowledging their efforts. Butterflies appeared in unusual numbers, settling on the new plants as if to bless them.

Maggie sought to break the silence. "They say you can't really know a place until you've got dirt under your nails from its soil. Do you feel it, Emily? The way the earth's waking up under our hands?" She smiled warmly, her eyes twinkling with the wisdom of someone who had spent her life nurturing both plants and people.

Emily smiled, brushing a lock of hair from her face. "Absolutely, it's like the soil remembers you, welcomes you back every time you dig in." Her fingers brushed over the soft earth, a sense of calm settling over her. "This garden...it's like an old friend coming back to life with me." She paused, her voice taking on a softer tone, almost as if speaking to herself. "I forgot what it was like to be needed by something, to have a purpose like this."

Usually reserved, Alex nodded as he dug a small hole for a plant. "Yeah, working with wood or working with soil...it's all about knowing the cycles. Keeps you grounded, literally and figuratively." He gave a small chuckle, patting down the soil around a newly planted sapling. "Dad used to say, 'A good plank of wood and a good patch of earth have a lot in common. They both need respect, patience and just the right touch.' Looks like this patch is getting all that and more." He glanced up, catching Emily's eye. His tone was light, but there was a sincerity there, a shared understanding of the quiet, steady work that both woodworking and gardening required.

Speaking softly, Liam told them about the plants. "Every leaf here holds a whisper, every root a memory," the mystical guide murmured, his hands moving as if in a dance with the soil. "Your grandmother could hear them, Emily. And now, I think you're hearing them too." His words were almost poetic, filled with a reverence that suggested he saw the garden as more than just a plot of land but a living, breathing entity with its own secrets. "She knew this garden was alive in more ways than one." He paused as if waiting for the garden itself to respond, his eyes closing for a moment, listening to some unspoken rhythm only he seemed to hear.

More pragmatic but equally invested, Alex added, "And it's not just about the planting. It's also making sure these plants get what they need to thrive—water, sunlight, and a bit of love." He winked at Emily, his usual reserved demeanor softening for a moment. "You can't just plant a seed and expect it to grow without care. Same goes for us, I guess." He laughed, the sound almost lost in the rustling leaves, but there was a warmth to it that hinted at a deeper understanding, a shared experience of nurturing growth, both in the garden and in their own lives.

The conversation flowed easily, bridged by Emily's gentle probing. "So, Alex, Maggie tells me you're quite the handyman. What got you into that line of work?"

Alex chuckled, patting down the soil around a new plant. "My dad was a carpenter. I grew up with sawdust in my hair. Guess it was inevitable I'd follow in his footsteps." There was a hint of pride in his voice and a softness, as if he were remembering the gentle moments spent learning his craft.

Finding an unexpected common ground in their shared appreciation for the healing power of nature, Emily said, "Liam, your connection to the plants is something else. I can't imagine doing this without either of you."

"It's all about balance," he replied, patting down the soil around a new plant. "The mystical and the practical coming together. That's what makes a garden, or any project, really come to life." His tone was almost meditative as if he were sharing a quiet wisdom rather than making a statement.

Alex nodded; his approach was always grounded. "Exactly. And speaking of life, look at this garden now compared to when we started. It's like it's breathing again, thanks to your vision, Emily."

Touched by their words, she reflected on the progress they'd made. "It's more than I could have achieved alone. This garden needed all of us, our different strengths." She looked around at her friends, her voice filled with gratitude. "I think that's what makes it special. It's not just my project anymore—it's ours."

"And Emily," Maggie turned, her eyes twinkling. "I've seen you with that camera of yours. Your photographs capture Blue Ridge Haven's spirit beautifully. What draws you to photography?"

"It's the stories," she replied, her voice passionate. "Every person, every landscape has a story to tell. Photography lets me share those stories, capture moments that might otherwise be lost." Her eyes wandered over the garden, the shadows lengthening in the late afternoon sun. "Just like this place. Every corner has a story, a memory of my grandmother, and now...now it has fresh stories, new memories, because of all of you."

Barriers dissolved to be replaced by budding friendships as they worked and talked. Their shared laughter and stories wove through the air, intertwining with the sound of birds and the rustle of the leaves. The garden, which had once seemed like an overwhelming burden, was now a place of connection and growth—not just for the plants but for all of them.

Maggie's glance lingered on Emily. "It's not just the garden that brought you back to Blue Ridge Haven, is it?"

The question hung in the air, and Emily paused, her hands still. The warmth of the sun and the earthy scent comforted her as she gathered her thoughts. "No, it wasn't just the garden," she confessed, her voice tinged with vulnerability and relief. "Back in the city, I was teaching creative writing. Trying to inspire my students to find their voices, to tell their stories. But somewhere along the way, I lost my own."

She glanced at the seedlings they had just planted, their potential for growth mirroring her own. "I needed a break, a change from the constant cycle of semesters, from the endless clinic visits and the disappointment that followed each one. But that's another story. The garden...my grandmother's legacy offered me a chance for something different. A chance to heal, to find my voice again in a place that always felt like home."

Liam, Alex, and Maggie listened, understanding dawning in their eyes. The garden had brought them together, but their shared experiences, struggles, and hopes forged a deeper connection.

"Restoring this garden is my way of finding a new path," Emily continued, her gaze sweeping over the lush green around them. "It's about creating something beautiful, not just in the soil, but in life. It's about healing and new beginnings for all of us."

"Look at us," Maggie said, stepping back to admire their work. "Brought together by a garden and a handful of seeds. We've got a good thing going here. It's not just the garden that's growing. I think we all are, in our own ways."

Glancing around her, then at her new friends, Emily said, "This started as a project to reconnect with my grandmother's legacy, but it's more than just a garden, isn't it? It's about us, too, our growth and what we bring to each other's lives."

Agreeing, Liam smiled. "It's a reminder that from the smallest seeds, grow the most beautiful flowers."

"And what about you, Liam? You've shared so much about the plants, but we know little about you," Maggie said.

He paused, his hand stilling over the soil. "There's not much to tell," he drawled. "I've wandered these lands for as long as I can remember, learning from the earth and the creatures that inhabit it. The garden called to me, just as it did to all of you."

Sensing there was more to Liam's story, something he was keeping hidden, Emily didn't press. "Well, we're glad you're here. Your knowledge is invaluable."

Their chatter filled the garden, a celebration of new connections and the promise of growth. As the sun set, painting the sky with hues of orange and pink, a sense of peace settled over Emily. In this garden, she was planting the seeds of her future, nurtured by the friendship and hope that bloomed around her. She looked at Maggie, Liam, and Alex, who were also admiring their handiwork, their faces alight with satisfaction and a hint of tiredness.

"You know," Emily started, her voice warm with the offer she was about to make, "I can't thank you enough for all the help today. How about I make us dinner? Nothing fancy, just some sandwiches and gazpacho I have chilling in the refrigerator. It's the least I can do."

Maggie, who pulled off her garden gloves, and Alex, who was cleaning some tools, both agreed eagerly. "That sounds wonderful. It's been a long time since I've shared a good, home-cooked meal with friends," Maggie said.

"I'm in," Liam accepted, leaning on his shovel. "You've turned this place into a little paradise, Emily. And the best part is the company."

Leaving their tools behind, the group made their way into the farmhouse. The kitchen's rustic charm welcomed them like an old friend. As Emily prepared the meal, the simplicity of the task allowed for the conversation to flow even more freely. The kitchen filled with the aroma of the gazpacho and the sound of laughter, a testament to the bonds being forged over shared work and now, a shared meal.

"What can I help with?" Maggie asked as she watched Emily move around the kitchen, gathering ingredients for the sandwiches.

"Here is the bread, condiments, meat, and cheese. Why don't you all make your sandwiches while I dish up the soup?" Emily took some bowls from the cabinet as the others prepared their sandwiches. She placed four bowls of gazpacho on the table.

Sitting down to eat, the glow of the day's accomplishments reflected in their faces. The meal, simple in its ingredients but rich in meaning, symbolized the new friendships and the renewed sense of purpose each had found in the garden.

"I was thinking," Emily began, her eyes alight with enthusiasm, "about planting a mix of perennials and annuals. Something that ensures year-round color. What do you think?" Her excited tone reflected her hopes for the garden's future.

Nodding thoughtfully, Liam added, "How about integrating some native plants? They're good for the environment and attract pollinators. I can help select a few that would thrive here."

Maggie's face lit up with a smile. "And let's not forget a little corner for herbs. There's nothing like fresh basil or rosemary from your own garden."

"My first attempt at gardening was a disaster. I thought plants needed as much water as possible. Turned out, you can love them too much." There was a warmth to Alex's laughter, a recognition of his own growth as much as the garden's.

"You've come a long way, Alex." Emily laughed as Maggie and Liam joined in. "I never thought I'd get this far with it, but now...I can't imagine letting it go. It's funny how things take root, isn't it?"

Their conversation that evening, woven through with laughter and moments of contemplation, marked the beginning of a deep and enduring friendship. It wasn't just a garden they were nurturing but a shared dream of renewal and connection.

6

ROOTS AND RECOGNITION

Emily's morning began with a purposeful stroll through Blue Ridge Haven, the town still awakening under the soft glow of the morning sun. Her steps led her to the local garden center, a place brimming with life and the earthy scent of promise. As she meandered through aisles of colorful blooms and verdant greenery, her thoughts were on envisioning the garden's transformation with each plant she considered. No longer just a project, the garden was a return to the magic and joy she had known as a child, a way to reconnect with the legacy her grandmother had left behind.

A hub for the community's plant enthusiasts, the garden center quickly became a stage for unexpected reunions. Word of Emily's return and her ambitious project had spread via the small town's grapevine. Faces, both new and familiar, expressed their admiration and support for her undertaking while greeting her.

"Emily Hawthorne, as I live and breathe! Heard you were back in town," came a cheerful greeting from Mrs. Dalton, her grandmother's longtime friend. "Restoring Cora's garden, are you? That place was the talk of the town once upon a time."

Another encounter brought a young couple, new to Blue Ridge Haven, who had heard about her project from Maggie. "We're garden enthusiasts ourselves," they said, their eyes bright with excitement. "It's inspiring to see someone invest in bringing beauty back to the community. Count us in if you need extra hands."

As these interactions unfolded, Emily sensed a deepening connection between Blue Ridge Haven and its residents. It seemed that her grandmother's legacy had left an indelible mark on the town, and now Emily was becoming part of that continuing story. With each interaction, her resolve strengthened, her vision for the garden expanding beyond its physical boundaries to touch the lives of those around her. She started to leave the garden center, not just with a collection of plants but with a sense of belonging and a community eager to see the garden—and Emily—flourish.

A familiar figure was examining a collection of fruit trees. His concentration on the plants before him mirrored his dedicated work in her grandmother's garden.

"Alex!" Emily called out, her voice bridging the distance between them.

He looked up, a smile breaking across his face. "Emily! Didn't expect to see you here. Looking for new plants?"

"Yes, exactly," she replied, joining him by the fruit trees. "I'm thinking of adding some variety. What about you?"

"I'm here for the same reason. Thought some fruit trees might bring a new life to the garden," Alex said, gesturing toward a small apple tree. "Imagine picking fresh fruit from your backyard a few years from now."

Their conversation flowed easily from there, discussing potential plants, sharing ideas, and even debating the merits of various tree species. The chance meeting solidified their bond over the shared project and highlighted their growing friendship, rooted in a mutual love for gardening and the community.

"Well, imagine finding you two here."

Both turned to see Liam approaching with a wide smile, his arms filled with various gardening supplies. There was something ethereal about him today, an almost imperceptible glow surrounding him, his presence serene and unearthly.

"Just the person we need," Emily said, her enthusiasm evident. "We were just discussing what plants to get. Any thoughts on fruit trees?"

"Absolutely," Liam replied, setting down his supplies. "I was actually reading up on some dwarf varieties that could work beautifully. They don't take up much space and still produce plenty of fruit."

"That sounds perfect," Alex agreed, nodding appreciatively.

The trio moved toward the fruit tree section, where Liam pointed out a few species known for their hardiness and suitability for the local climate. "These apple and pear trees could be a real highlight," he suggested. "And they're fantastic for attracting wildlife."

They wandered through the aisles. Emily noticed a few unusual plants that seemed to shimmer with an inner light, their leaves whispering secrets as she passed. A twinge of excitement overcame her, recognizing these plants from her grandmother's stories about the magical flora that thrived in the enchanted gardens.

"Look at these," she said, pointing to a cluster of luminescent flowers. "Grandma used to tell me about plants like these. She said fairies touched them and had special properties."

Liam's eyes twinkled with interest. "I've heard about these. They're said to enhance the growth of other plants and bring a sense of tranquility to the garden."

The conversation shifted smoothly from fruit trees to strategies for organic pest control, with Liam providing insightful tips he had learned from years of experience. Emily listened intently, her notebook in hand, jotting down every piece of advice. She noticed how Liam's presence seemed to draw her out of her internal musings and connect her to the immediate world around her. His passion for nature and its cycles was infectious, and she became increasingly captivated—not just by the plants but by Liam's perspective on life.

"It's fascinating how everything in nature is interconnected," he said, gesturing toward a group of pollinator-friendly shrubs. "Just like human relationships, don't you think? Sometimes, it takes a bit of nurturing and a lot of patience to see growth."

His words struck a chord in her. She glanced at Liam, his profile outlined against the lush greenery of the garden center, and sensed a pang of something she couldn't quite place. Was it admiration or something deeper? Emily wondered if her feelings for Mark had ever sparked such a reaction. This blend of respect and introspection.

Liam laughed softly at something Alex said. Emily's thoughts drifted to Mark and their relationship. Over time, what was once a safe harbor—and especially through the trials of attempting to start a family—seemed more like a recurring cycle of hope and disappointment. With Liam, however, discussion about growth and recovery was laden with optimism, not burdened by past failures.

She considered how Liam's view of the garden as a space of renewal and a source of continuous learning mirrored the lessons she was slowly accepting about her own life and relationships. Perhaps this was the perspective she needed to apply to her relationship with Mark.

"I really believe this garden could be a place of healing," Liam continued, pulling Emily back from her contemplation.

"Yes, I think so too," she agreed, her voice steadier than she felt. "There's so much potential here. Not just for the plants, but for us, for everyone involved."

With palpable energy and feeding off each other's passion and excitement, they filled their carts with plants and gardening tools. It wasn't just about beautifying a space; it was about creating a sustainable, living ecosystem, much like the relationships they were cultivating.

Liam proposed a visit to a nearby botanical garden for more inspiration. "They have an amazing herb garden that could give us some ideas," he mentioned. "What do you think about a field trip next weekend?"

Emily and Alex agreed enthusiastically, both pleased with the opportunity to learn more and strengthen their collaborative effort.

Leaving the garden center together, plans and plants in tow, a renewed sense of excitement for the garden's future thrilled her. This unexpected encounter with Alex and Liam underscored the serendipitous nature of her journey back to Blue Ridge Haven and the surprising connections that were helping to steer her path.

Liam had also unintentionally helped her see her feelings for Mark in a new light. It wasn't just about whether they could reconcile. It was about understanding what she truly needed from a relationship—connection, presence, and growth, much like what she experienced when discussing plans with Liam and Alex.

Walking back through Blue Ridge Haven, she saw the town with fresh eyes. The beauty of the mountains, the vibrancy of the streets, and the warmth of the people reminded her why her grandmother had loved this place so dearly. In that moment, she knew she wasn't just restoring a garden; she was nurturing the roots of her own place in the world, intertwined with the community that had welcomed her back with open arms. She also knew there were conversations she needed to have and decisions she needed to make. Thanks to Liam's unwitting guidance, she was more equipped to face those challenges, knowing that just like the garden, she too was capable of regeneration.

7

THE BOTANICAL ESCAPE

The morning air buzzed with excitement as Emily, Liam, Alex, and Maggie gathered at the entrance to the local botanical garden. The sun shone across the meticulously landscaped grounds, and the smell of blooming flowers hung thick in the air, mingling with an almost ethereal aroma that seemed to shimmer with magic.

"Well, isn't this a sight for sore eyes?" Maggie exclaimed, her silver hair shimmering in the light. Her gaze traveled over the vibrant displays and neat paths winding between diverse plant collections, some that seemed to glow faintly as if imbued with their own light.

"It's stunning," Emily agreed, a note of anticipation in her voice. "I can't wait to see what ideas we can bring back for Grandmother's garden."

Their unofficial guide led the way, pointing out notable plants and enthusiastically sharing snippets of information. "This area is devoted to native plants of the region," Liam said, gesturing toward a lush section with wildflowers and hardy shrubs that seemed to whisper secrets as the breeze rustled their leaves. "We could take inspiration from this setup for the borders."

Alex nodded, his gaze following Liam's gestures. "The mix of textures and colors is incredible. Imagine how beautiful something like this would look next to Cora's old farmhouse."

Maggie wandered farther down the path, her interest piqued by a collection of medicinal plants. "Oh, this could be our healing corner!" she called back to the group. "We could have a similar arrangement near the back of the garden."

Liam joined her, noting the calming effect of the lavender and chamomile swaying in the breeze. "It's soothing just to stand here," he remarked. "A healing corner could be the perfect addition."

They continued their stroll, and Emily noticed a series of tiny, luminescent orbs floating just above the ground, flitting among the flowers. She paused, watching as one orb settled on a petal, revealing itself as a small, delicate fairy with wings glowing like a firefly's tail.

"Look at that," she whispered, her eyes wide with wonder. "The fairies here are so beautiful."

Maggie smiled, her gaze following Emily's. "This garden is truly enchanting. The fairies help the plants grow and ensure the harmony of this place. Just like in your grandmother's garden."

Emily snapped a photo of the arrangement with her phone, her mind whirling with possibilities. "Imagine a cozy seating area surrounded by these plants," she mused. "It could be a peaceful retreat for anyone needing a moment of solace."

They moved on, admiring intricate rock gardens, serene water features, and lush greenhouses brimming with exotic species. Every corner of the botanical garden seemed to echo with familiar magic, one that reminded her of her grandmother's. Suddenly, something caught her eye—a small plaque nestled among a bed of vibrant roses near a wrought-iron gate.

Drawn to it, Emily stepped away from the group and knelt down to read the inscription. The bronze plaque was simple but elegant, its lettering partially obscured by leaves that had grown around it. She gently brushed them aside, revealing the words:

In Loving Memory of Cora Wren—For Her Generous Contributions and Dedication to the Growth of This Garden. Her Plants, Her Time, Her Heart.

A lump formed in Emily's throat, and her eyes misted as she read the plaque again. She hadn't known this part of her grandmother's history—that she had been involved with this botanical garden, sharing not just plants but also her passion for nature.

"Emily?" Maggie's voice called softly behind her. "Everything okay?"

Emily turned, blinking back tears as she smiled. "Look," she said, stepping aside to let the others see. "It's a plaque for my grandmother. I did not know she had a connection to this place."

Leaning in to read it, Maggie's face softened. "Your grandmother was a remarkable woman. It doesn't surprise me she left her mark here, too."

Alex placed a reassuring hand on Emily's shoulder. "She must have loved this garden as much as her own."

"It makes sense." Liam nodded thoughtfully. "She understood the power of plants, of growth and renewal. Her spirit is very much alive in this place."

Warmth and a deep connection to her grandmother that seemed to span time and space surged through Emily. "I wish I had known," she whispered. "But it seems right, finding this now. Like she's still guiding me, showing me the way."

The group fell silent, sharing the moment with Emily as they stood by the plaque. It was as if Cora herself was with them, her presence woven into the very fabric of their surroundings.

After a few moments, Maggie gently broke the silence. "Your grandmother would be so proud of what you're doing with her garden. She's here with you, every step of the way."

Emily nodded, wiping her eyes. "Thank you, Maggie. I feel her here, in this garden, and in every seed we plant back home."

They strolled farther along the paths, the discovery of the plaque adding a layer of meaning to their visit. The botanical garden seemed to unveil new marvels at every turn, igniting their imaginations and offering endless inspiration.

By mid-morning, the four friends rested on a shaded bench in front of the charming coffee shop nestled amid the greenery. Its stone façade and flowering window boxes beckoned them inside. The aroma of freshly brewed coffee wafted through the air, mingling with the floral scents from the surrounding blooms.

"How about we take a break?" Emily suggested with a smile. "My treat."

The others agreed enthusiastically and followed her into the cozy shop, where the warm ambiance and rustic wooden tables promised a relaxing respite.

Liam scanned the menu overhead. "I'm tempted to try the lavender latte."

"Same here," Alex said, nodding appreciatively at the selection of unique drinks. "It sounds perfect for a day like this."

Maggie opted for the chamomile tea, her eyes lighting up at the idea. "Chamomile is calming, and I think we could all use a bit of that."

Emily placed their order at the counter, adding a cappuccino for herself, and soon the four friends were seated at a sunlit table beside a wide window overlooking the blooming garden beyond.

"This place is wonderful," Maggie remarked, cradling her warm tea. "It's a little haven all its own."

Liam took a sip of his latte and sighed contentedly. "And the drinks are excellent. There's a subtle hint of lavender that makes it feel special."

"I love the way it blends with the garden theme," Emily said, glancing around at the potted herbs and floral arrangements decorating the shop. "It's all so thoughtful."

They chatted amiably, sharing ideas for Cora's garden and discussing their morning's inspirations. When they finally finished their drinks, they lingered a while longer, savoring the calming atmosphere and the joy of friendship.

"This was such a wonderful idea," Alex said as they stood. "Thank you for the treat, Emily."

She smiled warmly. "Anytime. I think we all needed a little boost." She couldn't help but think how she and Mark would have loved to have a place like this to visit and spend time together on one of their lazy Sunday mornings. She missed those times.

"This place is magical," Maggie breathed. "It's easy to lose yourself here, surrounded by so much beauty."

"Agreed," Alex replied. "It's like stepping into another world."

Liam crossed his arms thoughtfully. "The beauty of a garden like this is that it offers something for everyone. A place to connect with nature, find inspiration, or simply unwind."

Emily smiled, her gaze scanning the vibrant scene before her. "I think we've found some wonderful ideas for our own little paradise."

They lingered in the garden until late afternoon, relishing the warm camaraderie and inspiration shared between them. As they finally made their way back to the entrance, their steps were lighter, their minds buzzing with plans for their own revitalization project.

"I can't wait to get back and start implementing some of these ideas," Emily said as they exited. "We could have our own botanical haven in no time."

Liam's eyes gleamed with determination. "Let's get to work then. There's no time like the present."

As the group arrived back at the farmhouse, the warm glow of the setting sun painted the garden with hues of amber and gold. Emily stepped onto the porch, her heart swelling with determination and gratitude for the day's discoveries. Her eyes were drawn to the familiar sight on the back porch—the handwoven basket neatly filled with packets of seeds.

She paused, the now expected yet still mysterious offering stirring a mix of curiosity and comfort within her. Every morning since her arrival, a basket just like this had appeared, replenished with seeds of all kinds—some familiar, some rare, all bearing an almost otherworldly vibrancy. She had assumed the basket was from her grandmother, a final gift left behind. But now, with each new morning, the mystery deepened.

"This wasn't full when we left," she said, holding up the basket as her friends gathered around. The scent of cedar and citrus blossoms filled the air.

Liam leaned in, inspecting the neatly packed seed packets. "It's as if someone knows exactly what your garden needs."

Maggie exchanged a glance with Alex. "It's almost as if the garden itself is sending you help," she said softly, her tone touched with awe.

Emily's fingers brushed the edges of the basket, her resolve hardening. "Whoever is leaving these, it feels...purposeful. Like they want this garden to thrive as much as we do."

She carried the basket inside, her thoughts dancing between wonder and possibility. Tomorrow, she would plant some of these seeds, weaving them into the fabric of the garden she was restoring. Whether by chance, magic, or design, she knew these seeds carried more than the promise of growth—they carried a message of hope.

8

CHALLENGES AND REFLECTIONS

The unexpected doorbell chime cut through the morning calm, pulling Emily from her thoughts. She hesitated for a moment, not expecting any visitors, then walked to the door. A messenger clad in the uniform of a local courier service greeted her with a polite nod. "Emily Hawthorne?" he asked, confirming her identity before handing over a sealed envelope. "Please sign here," he added, extending a digital pad toward her.

With a signature, the envelope was hers. The messenger offered a courteous, "Have a good day," before departing, leaving her with the weight of the delivery in her hands. The pleasant, formal manner of the exchange contradicted the personal storm that the contents of the envelope would unleash.

She broke the seal of the envelope and unfolded the papers. Despite the warmth of the morning sun streaming through the window, a chill ran through her. Each word she read was like a stone sinking in her stomach, the legal jargon starkly impersonal yet cutting deeply. The realization that Mark had initiated this ending that formalized their separation with such clinical precision, left her hollow.

It wasn't just the beginning of the end of their marriage. It was the dismantling of a shared life, of mutual dreams, now declared null and void on paper. A profound sense of isolation, as if the ground had shifted beneath her, leaving her adrift in the sea of uncertainty about her future, her identity, and her worth not only as a woman but as a person, settled on her. The papers in her hands symbolized not just a legal process but the closing of a chapter of her life that she had believed would last forever. A future that had included Mark.

The sun dipped lower as she sat quietly among the plants, the silent tears streaming down her face reflecting the turmoil within. The papers, an unyielding reminder of her crumbling marriage, lay forgotten beside her. Tiny, glowing orbs, like fireflies, appeared around her, their soft light flickering as if they were sharing her sadness.

"Emily?" Maggie called out as she made her way down the garden path, her approach gentle.

Seeing Maggie, she wiped away her tears. But the sight of her friend, the concern evident in her eyes, broke the last of her resolve. "I'm sorry, Maggie," she managed between sobs. "I thought I could handle this, but it's just...so hard."

Maggie sat beside her, her presence a comforting anchor. "Do you want to talk about it?"

Emily took a second to compose herself. "Mark made our separation legal today."

"I'm so sorry, Emily." Maggie patted her hand. "I saw the messenger this morning. I had no idea it would be such bad news." Her voice was sympathetic, her hand offering a gentle reassurance. "This must be such a shock."

"It's...it's not just that," The words tumbled out amid her tears. "it's the finality of it all. Mark and I, we built a life together, dreamed together. And now, it's as if all of that meant nothing. I have my career I worked hard for. I studied hard, did everything I was supposed to, and it worked out. Why can't it be that way with starting a family? I feel like such a failure."

"This has to be so difficult for you."

"This is my fault. He wants a family so bad. I can't give him one.

He deserves someone who can." Tears streamed down Emily's cheeks.

Maggie wrapped an arm around her shoulder. "It's not your fault, dear. You're not alone in this. You have people who care, people who will stand by you through the storms."

Emily looked around then back at Maggie. The garden seemed to pulse with a soft, reassuring glow, the tiny orbs of light hovering closer as if to offer their support. "I just don't know if I can do this on my own," she whispered, the vulnerability in her voice raw and evident.

"You won't have to," Maggie assured her, squeezing her hand. "I'll be here every step of the way. And this garden," she gestured around them, "it will heal you. It's not just plants and flowers growing here, Emily. It's you, too."

"Hey, Emily, I saw Maggie here. I thought I would drop by to see how the new blooms are doing...but it looks like you could use a friend," Liam said, his voice full of warmth.

Emily nodded, grateful for his timing. "Yeah, it's been a tough day," she admitted, glancing at Maggie. A strange mix of emotions hit Emily as Liam approached, concern etching his features. A small part of her was surprised.

How did he seem to know that something was wrong before even a word passed between them? But this surprise quickly gave way to profound relief. It was as if he had silently acknowledged her pain with no need for her to voice it, sparing her the effort of having to explain her distress.

A warm gratitude for his sensitivity filled her. His presence alone seemed to say that he was there for her, ready to offer support without pressing for details she might not be ready to share. This unspoken understanding made her appear seen and safe, enveloping her in a comfort that was as unexpected as it was needed.

Emily realized how rare and precious such a connection was. Liam's instinctive grasp of her emotional state, his choice to offer solace through action rather than words, tied a gentle bond of trust between them.

He crouched beside her, his presence soothing. "I don't know what's wrong, but I know nature has a way of healing, of pushing through the toughest soil to bloom again."

She listened, and as Liam spoke, the surrounding garden wasn't so oppressive. His words reminded her of cycles and seasons, of renewal that follows even the harshest winters. The glowing orbs seemed to dance in agreement, casting a magical light over them.

Her mind drifted back to a simpler time, to her childhood spent in this very garden with her grandmother, Cora. She remembered a particular day when she was upset because her mother insisted she come home a day early. Grandmother Cora had taken her small hand in hers, leading her to a secluded part of the garden where the air always seemed a little warmer, the colors a little brighter.

"Emily, my dear," Cora had said, her voice like a gentle breeze, "this garden is a special place. It's alive with magic, just like you. When you're sad or lost, come here. Listen to the plants, feel the earth, and let it heal your heart."

Young Emily had sniffled, wiping her tears with the back of her hand. "But how, Grandmother?"

Cora smiled, kneeling down to Emily's level. "Just as plants need time to grow, so do our hearts need time to heal. Patience, love, and a bit of magic—that's the secret. Do you see those tiny lights?" She had pointed to the glowing orbs that floated around them. "They are the garden's way of comforting you, showing that you are never alone."

The memory faded, leaving Emily with a bittersweet nostalgia and a renewed sense of purpose. Seeing Liam's kind and understanding face, a connection to the garden, her grandmother, and the present moment washed through her.

He gestured toward a neglected corner where the light filtered through the trees in a way that seemed to invite quiet contemplation.

"What about starting a Healing Garden here, Emily? It could be a place dedicated to growth and recovery, filled with plants known for their therapeutic properties. Lavender for calmness, chamomile for soothing, and perhaps rosemary for remembrance," he suggested, his eyes reflecting a vision of tranquility.

"The garden could have winding paths, with benches tucked away where people can sit and just be. It's about creating a space that helps anyone who walks through be lighter by the time they leave," Liam continued, his voice soft yet filled with an infectious passion.

Emily looked at the space, visualizing his idea. The concept of a garden that could help mend her broken spirits while offering the same possibility of renewal to others resonated deeply with her. "I love that idea. It's something positive to focus on, a way to channel all this...into something that can bring peace."

She found her thoughts shifting as the conversation flowed. The sharp edges of her sadness softening into something more akin to resolve. With Maggie's compassion and Liam's gentle encouragement, hope flickered inside her. A sense that even amid her personal upheaval, growth was possible.

9

ECHOES OF THE PAST

The sun began its descent, which Emily considered a reflection of her journey. The beauty of the blooming flowers contrasted with the turmoil churning inside her as she stared at the papers laid out on the wooden table in front of her. Each word on the page was like a leaf falling from a tree, signaling the end of a season.

Taking a deep breath, she picked up her phone. Her fingers hovered over the call button next to Mark's name. A name that had once signified her partner, her confidante. Now, it was a bridge to a past filled with both joy and sorrow. The decision to call was difficult, but the need for closure and understanding outweighed her fear of reopening old wounds.

"Emily?" Mark's voice carried surprise and caution.

"Hi, Mark," her voice was steadier than she seemed. "I...we need to talk about the divorce papers."

There was a pause, a breath held between two worlds. "Okay," he finally said. "I'm listening."

She took a moment to gather her thoughts. "Why now, Mark? After all this time, why did you decide to file for divorce? I thought this time apart was to give us a chance to think about what we wanted and to work through everything."

His sigh traveled through the phone line like a shiver. "I guess...I was stuck, Emily. *We* were stuck. After everything with the fertility treatments, the silence between us grew too heavy. Neither one of us is happy. I thought this was a way for both of us to find a place of peace."

Listening to Mark, she perceived the weight of their shared pain. "I sensed that silence too," she admitted. "I just never thought...I hoped we could find our way back to each other."

She moved outside, where the evening breeze carried whispers of a world moving forward as Emily listened. Mark's voice offered a window into his soul, a soul she once knew better than her own.

"It wasn't an easy decision," he began, his words heavy with an emotion that time had not faded. "After everything, it's like we're living in a loop of pain and disappointment. I can't see a way out, and it seems like we're only hurting each other more by holding on." He paused. "I guess I think we're meant to find happiness, but not together. Like our paths have diverged, and I'm holding you back from finding a peace that I can't give you. The silence between us. It's not just the absence of words, Emily. It's the absence of us, of who we used to be to each other. I knew when you told me you were leaving, it was time."

Her heart ached, understanding and sorrow mingling within her.

Mark continued, "I thought about the dreams we shared, the life we envisioned when we married. And then, I looked at where we are —strangers under the same roof, mourning not just the children we can't have but the love that's somehow slipped through our fingers. The divorce papers...they weren't meant to erase what we had. They're my way of saying I love you enough to let you go, to hope that you can find a way to heal, to be happy. I realize that our love isn't the kind that lasts a lifetime in the way we expect but one that teaches us, changes us, and then sets us free. I'll always love you, Emily."

Tears streamed down her cheeks, not just for losing what they had but for the profound love that Mark's words conveyed. A love that sought her happiness above his own, a love brave enough to let go. To release them both from promises they'd made to each other but couldn't bring to fruition.

His voice was a soft echo as he concluded, "I filed for divorce not because I stopped loving you, Emily, but because I believed it was the most loving thing I could do for both of us. It was the hardest decision of my life, but I made it hoping someday we'd both find the peace and happiness we deserved, even if it's not together."

Their call ended, and she sat in reflective silence, the surrounding garden bathed in the soft glow of twilight. Mark's reasons for filing for divorce—a mix of love, loss, and the hope for new beginnings—resonated with her deeply. She realized their journey together had ended, but it was an end that came from a place of love and mutual respect. And with this understanding, she recognized the first correct step toward healing and moving forward, her heart open to the possibilities ahead.

Emily held the phone. Her heart ached with an uproar of emotions. She was torn between the past filled with love and dreams and the stark reality of their present. Mark's voice, once a source of comfort, now carried words that seemed to finalize the end of their relationship.

In the silence that followed the call, she sat motionless, the phone pressed against her chest, absorbing the finality of his words. His confession—that their parting ways were out of love and a desire for their happiness—was kind, but it was a kindness that pained her deeply. It suggested not just an end but an acknowledgment that their paths had diverged with no hope for reversal.

Enjoying the cool breeze of the evening, her mind replayed the years of their struggle together, the moments of silent meals, the unspoken frustrations, and the isolation within their shared space that had grown like a vine, slowly and persistently. Mark's words, "We are only hurting each other more by holding on," echoed in her thoughts, and she realized how much of herself she had been holding back in those silent moments, hoping for a change that never came.

The garden's thriving life and natural cycles stood in stark contrast to the stagnation she had experienced in her marriage. It reminded her that life, like the garden, required tending, and sometimes, the hardest decisions brought about the most fruitful outcomes. The divorce, though painful, was perhaps another form of pruning, necessary and ultimately leading to growth.

Twilight deepened, and Emily's initial shock gave way to a sorrowful clarity. She understood that letting go was not a failure but an act of great courage and love. It was a painful yet liberating truth she needed to embrace to move forward.

With a deep, slow breath, she rose from the garden bench. The night was filled with the sounds of life. The chirping of crickets, the rustle of leaves in the gentle wind. Each sound seemed to affirm that the world was moving on, and so could she. With each step back toward the house, she sensed a slight easing of the weight she had been carrying. Her path was uncertain, and the night stretched dark before her, but the garden, with its enduring cycles of decline and rebirth, reminded her she too was capable of rebirth.

She knew the road ahead would be wrought with challenges, but a fragile sense of hope revealed itself for the first time since receiving the papers. She would grieve for her lost love and the shared dreams that would never come to fruition, but she would allow herself to heal. To rediscover her own dreams and perhaps find new reasons to bloom.

A faint glow emanated from the corner of the garden as she approached the house. Curious, she walked over and found a cluster of night-blooming flowers she hadn't seen before. Their petals glowed with a soft, ethereal light, and as she leaned closer, she could hear a faint, melodic hum—an enchanting lullaby from the fairies. These flowers, she realized, were a gift from the garden, a symbol of hope and renewal.

She touched one of the glowing petals, and a sense of peace washed over her. The garden was not just a place of physical beauty. It was a realm of magic and healing. And in this magical sanctuary, she found the strength to believe in new beginnings.

10

THE DREAMER'S GARDEN

The quiet night was wrapped in a blanket of stars that twinkled above the farmhouse. After her conversation with Mark and the discovery of the glowing flowers in the garden, a deep weariness settled over Emily. The emotions of the day had left her drained, and all she wanted was to find some semblance of peace in the night's stillness.

The familiar scent of lavender and aged wood welcomed her as she stepped into the farmhouse, a comforting reminder she was home. The house, though quiet, seemed to hum with an energy she couldn't quite place as if it was aware of the turmoil she carried within her. She made her way upstairs to the bedroom, each step echoing softly in the silence.

She was immediately drawn to the small, worn doll propped up against the pillows. Rosie, a faithful companion, was a comforting presence. Emily had thought little about the doll's significance since she found it again, but tonight, its presence was more meaningful than ever.

She kept glancing at Rosie as she slipped into her nightgown, her mind swirling with memories. Her grandmother had always known how to make the darkest days seem brighter, and Rosie had been part of that magic. Emily could almost hear her grandmother's comforting voice as she remembered the countless times as a child when she would run to her grandmother with scraped knees or a heavy heart. Her grandmother would gently place Rosie in her arms, telling her that the doll held a special love that could chase away any sadness.

"Rosie will take care of you, just like she did for me," her grandmother would say, her voice full of warmth. "She knows all about the little things that make you happy. Just hold her close, and you'll see."

Those words, spoken with such certainty, had always brought Emily a sense of calm. Rosie wasn't just a toy. She was a vessel of joy, a reminder of the love and care that her grandmother had poured into her life. Holding Rosie always comforted her, as if the doll carried a piece of her grandmother's spirit.

She held the doll close as she climbed into bed. The familiar fabric, worn soft from years of being held, soothed her. She placed the doll beside her on the pillow, just like she used to when she was a little girl, and pulled the quilt up around her.

Lying in the darkness, the weight of her conversation with Mark pressed heavily on her chest. Though filled with love and a desire for her happiness, his words had cut deep. The finality of their parting, the acknowledgment that their paths had gone in different directions, was almost too much to bear. Emily closed her eyes, willing herself to find sleep, but her thoughts refused to quiet.

She reached out instinctively, her fingers brushing against Rosie's small hand. The touch was a simple, familiar comfort, and she let out a slow breath, allowing herself to relax. In the quiet moments before sleep, her mind drifted back to her childhood, to the times when the world seemed simpler, and Rosie was her confidante.

She remembered the summer evenings when she and her grandmother would sit on the porch, Rosie nestled in her lap, watching the sun set behind the mountains. Her grandmother would tell her stories of magic and wonder, of gardens that could heal hearts and dolls that brought dreams to life. Those stories had always left Emily with a sense of wonder, making her believe that anything was possible as long as she had Rosie by her side.

Her grandmother gave Rosie to her the day her parents left her at the farmhouse for the summer. She cried herself to sleep, missing them terribly. Rosie had been with her through all the milestones since then—the first day of school, when she was too nervous to speak to anyone, the nights when she'd lie awake, listening to the sounds in the dark, and thinking the world was too big and scary. In all those moments, Rosie was a constant source of comfort and reassurance.

Now, as an adult, with the weight of her own struggles bearing down on her, Emily realized how much she had missed that comfort. She hadn't thought about Rosie in years, hadn't needed her in the same way she had as a child. But tonight, as she lay in bed with her world seeming so uncertain, she was grateful for the small doll's presence.

She lay there on the edge of sleep. A strange sensation washed over her—a warmth, subtle and gentle, like the embrace of a loved one. It wasn't anything she could pinpoint, just a comforting presence that seemed to fill the room. She didn't open her eyes, afraid that the feeling would disappear if she did. Instead, she allowed herself to sink deeper into the warmth, letting it carry her to sleep.

Her dreams that night were vivid. She walked through the garden, more alive and vibrant than she had ever seen it. Flowers in every shade imaginable bloomed around her, their petals glowing softly in the moonlight. The air was thick with the scent of jasmine, wrapping her in a cocoon of tranquility.

Moving through the garden, she sensed a presence beside her—gentle, familiar, and comforting. She didn't look to see who or what it was; she didn't need to. The presence was enough to make her safe as if she was exactly where she was meant to be.

She reached out to touch the flowers. Their petals soft against her fingertips. There was magic here. She knew it in her bones, the same magic her grandmother had always spoken of.

The first rays of sunlight were just beginning to peek through the window when she woke the next morning. For a moment, she lay still, letting the remnants of the dream linger in her mind. There was a peace within her that hadn't been there the night before, a quiet reassurance that everything would be okay.

Emily turned her head, her eyes falling on Rosie, still beside her on the pillow. She smiled softly, reaching out and gently touching the doll's hand. "Thank you," she whispered, though she wasn't sure why she said it. Perhaps it was just the comfort Rosie had always brought her, or perhaps it was something more.

With renewed determination, Emily got out of bed and dressed for the day. The garden was waiting for her, ready to be brought back to life, and she was ready too. She knew the path ahead wouldn't be easy, but for the first time since arriving at the farmhouse, she knew she could face it.

She left Rosie on the bed, propped up against the pillows, and headed downstairs. The farmhouse was quiet and peaceful, as if it had also found its own calm. Emily stepped outside into the cool morning air, took a deep breath, noticed the earth beneath her feet, and smiled.

Like her heart, the garden was ready to bloom again, and Emily knew she had everything she needed to help it flourish.

As she turned to step off the porch, something caught her eye—the basket, once again, resting on the top step. She knelt, her fingers brushing against its rough woven edge. Inside were small packets of seeds, neatly labeled in handwriting she didn't recognize *Sunflowers, Sweet Peas, Morning Glory.*

Emily glanced around the quiet yard, half expecting to see someone watching from the trees or the edge of the garden. But the space was empty, save for the soft hum of the morning breeze carrying the scent of cedar and citrus. Cradling the basket, she carried it down the steps and toward the garden. Whoever leaves these gifts had given her more than seeds; they'd given her a sense of connection, a whisper of encouragement. She didn't know who to thank for these gifts, but as she set the basket on the edge of the garden bed and knelt to examine its contents, she felt a swell of gratitude.

The soil was rich and ready. The seeds, just like the others, would find their home. And Emily—she would find hers, too.

11

SEEDS OF REFLECTION

The sun was beginning its descent, casting a warm, golden hue over the garden. Emily strolled along the newly tilled rows, her fingers brushing the tops of the young shoots and the tall grasses still lining the edges of the garden. The day had been productive—she had spent hours planting the seeds from the basket she'd found that morning on the porch, each packet a small promise of life yet to come. With each seed she pressed into the soil, she felt a quiet connection to whoever had left them, as if their unseen hand guided her work.

Yet, as the shadows grew longer and the soft rustle of the wind filled the air, the familiar ache in her chest returned—the emptiness left by Mark's absence.

She paused by the old oak tree, its branches arching overhead like a protective canopy. She closed her eyes, breathing in the scent of earth and leaves. This garden had always been a place of solace, a refuge from the world. But today, even its beauty couldn't quiet the storm of emotions inside her.

"Mind if I join you?" Liam's voice came softly from behind, breaking her reverie. He approached with his usual calm demeanor, his presence somehow grounding.

Emily opened her eyes and turned to him, offering a small smile. "Sure, I could use the company."

They walked side by side for a while in comfortable silence, the only sound the rustle of leaves in the evening breeze. Finally, Liam spoke, his voice gentle. "I noticed you seemed a bit off today. Want to talk about it?"

Emily hesitated, her gaze fixed on the path ahead. She wasn't sure if she wanted to open up, but there was something about Liam—a quiet understanding in his eyes—that made her feel safe. "It's just... everything," she began, her voice barely more than a whisper. "The garden, my grandmother's legacy, this town...it's all so much. And on top of that, the divorce papers arrived."

Liam nodded, his expression sympathetic. "I'm sorry to hear that. I know how much Mark meant to you."

She looked at him, surprised. "How do you know that?"

He gave a small smile, his eyes softening. "I see the way you talk about him. There's still a lot of love there."

Emily sighed, her shoulders sagging under the weight of her emotions. "I don't even know if that love is enough anymore. Mark wanted a family so badly, and I...I couldn't give that to him. I feel like I failed him, like I failed us."

Liam stopped walking and turned to face her. "You didn't fail, Emily. Sometimes, life doesn't go the way we planned, but that doesn't mean you're to blame."

His words were kind, but she shook her head, tears welling up in her eyes. "I just...I miss him. I miss the way he used to make me laugh, the way he always knew how to cheer me up when I was down. He had this way of making everything feel...right."

Liam nodded thoughtfully. "Did he ever surprise you with a picnic in the middle of a rainstorm?" he asked with a small smile.

Emily blinked, her eyes widening in surprise. "He did. How do you know about that?"

Liam chuckled softly. "A lucky guess. I bet he didn't let the rain stop him, and you ended up dancing in the downpour instead of eating."

She laughed despite herself, the memory bringing a smile to her face. "He was always so spontaneous, always knew how to make the best of things."

They continued walking, and Liam gestured to a small clearing up ahead. "Why don't we sit for a bit?" he suggested. "It's a delightful spot to watch the sunset."

Emily nodded, following him to the clearing. They sat down on the grass, the world around them bathed in the soft glow of twilight. For a while, neither of them spoke. Emily stared out at the horizon, her thoughts a tangled mess.

"You know," Liam said after a moment, "sometimes we forget why we fell in love. We get caught up in what's missing, what's not working, and we lose sight of what we had...what we still have."

Emily turned to look at him, her brow furrowing. "What do you mean?"

Liam smiled, his gaze thoughtful. "I mean that love isn't always about perfection. It's about finding someone who sees you for who you are, flaws and all, and still chooses to be with you. It's about the brief moments, the memories that make you smile, even when things are tough."

She was quiet for a moment, his words sinking in. She thought about Mark—about the way he used to bring her coffee in bed on lazy Sunday mornings, the way he'd listen to her ramble on about her day, the way he always made her feel safe. She had been so focused on their struggles, on what she couldn't give him, that she had forgotten about all the things they had shared.

"You remind me a lot of him, you know," she breathed, turning to Liam. "The way you're always so calm, so steady. He used to be like that. Always knew how to make me better, just like you do."

Liam smiled, but there was a hint of something else in his eyes—something deeper, almost sad. "I'm glad I can help, Emily. But remember, I'm not him. And what you have with him is special."

Emily nodded, her gaze dropping to her hands. "I know. It's just...sometimes, I wonder if I've lost that part of myself, the part that knew how to love so fully. I've been so consumed by everything that's happened. I don't know if I can ever get it back."

Liam reached out, his hand resting gently on hers. "You can. You just have to remember what it was like. Remember the love, the joy, the way he made you feel. It's still there, buried beneath the pain. But it's there."

She looked up at him, her eyes searching his. "How do you know?"

His smile was soft and knowing. "Because I've seen it. In the way you tend to this garden, in the way you speak about your grandmother, about Mark. You have a lot of love in you, Emily. You just need to find it again."

A tear slipped down her cheek, and she quickly wiped it away, nodding. "Thank you, Liam. I needed to hear that."

They sat in silence for a while longer, watching as the sun dipped below the horizon, the sky painted in shades of pink and orange. A weight lifted from her chest, a sense of clarity settling over her. She wasn't sure what the future held, but she knew one thing: she wasn't ready to give up on love. Not yet.

As they sat there, she thought about Mark, about all the things they had shared and all the things they could still have. Liam was right. Maybe there was still something worth fighting for.

The first stars twinkled in the night sky, and Emily let out a deep breath. A sense of peace washed over her. She wasn't sure where this journey would take her, but for the first time in a long time, she was on the right path.

Liam stood up, offering her a hand. "Come on," he said with a warm smile. "Let's head back. The garden still needs us."

Emily took his hand, pulling herself up. She looked around the garden, the soft glow of the fairy lights casting a magical light over the flowers and trees. She had a renewed sense of hope, a determination to keep moving forward, no matter what.

Gratitude washed over her as they walked side by side back to the farmhouse. For Liam, for this garden, and for the love she still felt for Mark—a love that, despite everything, she wasn't ready to let go of.

12

ROOTS OF THE COMMUNITY

Stepping into the Mountain Mist Yoga Haven for the first time, Emily was nervous. The studio, nestled in the heart of Blue Ridge Haven's Art District, exuded a warm, inviting glow. She needed this. Something to focus on besides Mark. She'd just started yoga classes before leaving the city. A friend suggested yoga to help her anxiety over her infertility, telling her it would bring inner peace. Inner peace was what she needed.

"Welcome to Mountain Mist," greeted Luna, the instructor, with a serene smile. "I'm glad you're here. Find a spot anywhere you like."

Emily chose a spot near the window, unrolled her mat, and sat down, trying to still her racing thoughts.

"Let's start with some deep breaths. Inhale the future, exhale the past." Luna's voice was calm and grounding.

Emily smiled, realizing she was going to need more than one inhale and exhale to rid her of her past.

While sipping on chamomile tea in the studio's cozy lounge after the class, two women, Susan and June, approached her, their lively chatter filling the room.

"You're new to class, aren't you?" Susan asked, her eyes twinkling with curiosity.

"Yes." Emily nodded. "I'm Emily Hawthorne."

"Hawthorne?" Susan placed her finger on her chin as she stared into the distance.

"My grandmother was Cora Wren." Emily helped her thought process.

"Oh, the old Wren farmhouse?" June chimed in.

"Right. I'm planning to restore her garden." Emily smiled.

"That's quite the project," June chuckled. "Are you going to have any trouble with the lot next door?"

"Trouble?" Emily's brow furrowed, a knot of worry forming in her stomach.

Susan leaned closer, lowering her voice. "Word is developers have their eyes on it. Could change the entire area if they get their way."

June nodded solemnly. "It's a real David and Goliath situation. But that garden of yours? It's more important to this community than you might think."

Susan nodded. "From what I understand, this development poses a significant threat to the local community's character. Developing the Henderson property could disrupt the historical landscape of the area."

"Why don't you check out the local market?" June suggested. "It's the perfect way to meet the heart and soul of Blue Ridge Haven. And who knows? You might find some allies for your garden project."

The seeds of a plan took root as Emily left the studio. The yoga class, meant to be a step toward personal healing, had unexpectedly connected her to the pulse of Blue Ridge Haven. The garden wasn't just her project anymore. It was a piece of the community's history, now under her care.

Emily's heart was heavy with mixed emotions as she left the Mountain Mist Yoga Haven. The warmth of the studio lingered on her skin, a stark contrast to the cool air that greeted her outside. Blue Ridge Haven's Art District, with its vibrant murals and bustling studios, was more alive than ever. Yet, her mind was preoccupied with the news about the Henderson lot. The threat of development loomed large, casting a shadow over her plans for the garden.

The Henderson property was more than just a parcel of land—it was a piece of Blue Ridge Haven's soul. Tucked between the edge of the Art District and the quiet charm of Cora's farmhouse, the lot had long stood as a buffer between the rustic tranquility of the area and the encroaching pace of modern development. Its sweeping meadow, dotted with wildflowers in the spring and summer and golden grasses in the fall, was a haven for birds, deer, and countless pollinators that flitted between its blooms and Emily's fledgling garden.

Beyond its natural beauty, the land carried a legacy of its own. The Hendersons, long-time friends of Grandmother Cora, had always kept the lot undeveloped, a quiet act of defiance against the tide of urban sprawl. For decades, it had hosted community picnics, impromptu art workshops, and even small outdoor concerts where the music mingled with the rustling of the leaves. It was a space where neighbors gathered to celebrate milestones or simply to connect under the wide-open sky—a space that bound the community together.

Walking through the winding streets, she found herself drawn to the river that flowed steadily, indifferent to the rapid changes encroaching upon the community it had nourished for centuries. She stood there, watching the water, and there was a kinship with the river. Like it, she was navigating through obstacles, trying to find her way.

Determined to not let the news deter her spirit, she attended the local market June mentioned. It was set in a picturesque square, surrounded by historic buildings that whispered tales of Blue Ridge Haven's rich past. The market was a kaleidoscope of colors and sounds. Stalls adorned with handcrafted jewelry, homemade preserves, and fresh produce dotted the space. Musicians strummed guitars, their melodies blending with the laughter and chatter of the crowd.

She mingled with the locals, and the powerful sense of community struck her. Everyone seemed to know each other, and they welcomed her with open arms. She introduced herself and shared her connection to the Wren farmhouse and her plans to restore the garden. The response was overwhelmingly positive. People offered their help, shared stories of Cora Wren's legendary green thumb, and expressed their concern over the development plans.

At one stall, she met an elderly gentleman named Elias, who had been a friend of Cora's. "Your grandmother had a gift," he said, his eyes twinkling. "Her garden was more than just a plot of land. It was a haven for many of us. It brought the community together, much like this market." His words resonated with Emily. She realized that the garden had the potential to be a unifying force for Blue Ridge Haven, a way to preserve its soul amid the creeping modernization.

Energized by the support, Emily outlined her vision for the garden. She imagined a space that honored Cora's legacy while serving as a community hub. A place where workshops could be held, where local artists could display their work, and where people could come together to share stories and skills. The garden would be a testament to Blue Ridge Haven's resilience, a piece of living history that would stand defiantly in the face of development. With each step, the sounds of the market seemed to buoy her spirits. The strum of the guitars carried a message of resilience and continuity.

Emily walked through the bustling local market. Each stall offered a feast for the eyes. Vivid arrays of handcrafted jewelry that glinted under the afternoon sun, stacks of colorful hand-woven baskets, and rows of jars filled with golden honey and rich, dark preserves. Emily reached out, her fingers brushing against the rough texture of a handcrafted scarf, the fabric dyed with the deep blues and purples of native wildflowers.

A burst of citrus from a stall selling organic lemons reminded her of Sunday mornings in the kitchen with Mark, where they'd squeeze fresh lemonade and plan their day. The memory brought a pang of longing. Mark would have loved this type of market, with its focus on craftmanship and local produce. She could almost hear his light-hearted teasing as he'd inevitably start bargaining with a vendor, his eyes twinkling with the joy of the simple interaction.

At another stall, she stopped to sample a piece of ripe peach, its juice bursting sweetly on her tongue. The flavor was so rich and sun-warmed it was like biting into summer itself. Mark had always raved about her peach pies, and for a moment, Emily wondered what it would be like to experience this market through his eyes. To share with him the joy of discovering each unique stall, to discuss how they might use these local treasures in their next culinary experiment.

But as she watched a young couple laugh, their arms laden with flowers and fresh vegetables, a bittersweet ache overcame her. She missed sharing these moments with Mark, yet she also sensed a deepening resolve. This market, this community—they were reasons to fight for the garden, to preserve the way of life that this place embodied. Her heart swelled with a mix of nostalgia and newfound determination. Mark had made the decision for her to end their marriage. She would protect this community and its traditions, not just for herself or her memories, but for everyone who called this place home.

The sun dipped lower, and the market slowly emptied. A profound connection to Blue Ridge Haven filled her. She had come in search of healing and peace but found so much more. The garden project, once a personal endeavor, had blossomed into a communal crusade. It was a chance to contribute to the fabric of the town, to weave her own story into its tapestry. Her stroll through the market helped her integrate her past with her present, using her memories to fuel her current actions and decisions. Serving as a bridge between who she was with Mark and who she was becoming on her own provided both comfort in her memories and strength in her new identity.

Emily left the market with a heart full of hope and a notebook brimming with ideas. She noticed something curious. The path seemed to shimmer slightly as if illuminated by an unseen light. Intrigued, she followed the shimmering trail leading her to a secluded corner of the market square. Hidden among the ordinary stalls was a small, enchanting booth covered with ivy and twinkling fairy lights. The sign above read Enchanted Seeds and Magical Plants.

A kindly older woman, her eyes sparkling with a knowing

wisdom, greeted Emily. "Welcome, dear. I've been expecting you," she said with a smile that hinted at secrets untold.

A strange yet comforting sensation filled her as if she had stepped into another world. "Expecting me?" she echoed, curious. A familiar scent wafted through the air.

The woman nodded. "Word travels fast in a place like Blue Ridge Haven, especially among those who tend to the earth. I hear you're restoring Cora Wren's garden."

"Yes, that's right," Emily replied, a sense of destiny in the air.

The older woman reached under the counter and pulled out a small pouch filled with seeds. "These are not ordinary seeds," she explained. "They carry the magic of the land, the same magic that your grandmother nurtured in her garden. Use them with care, and they will help your garden flourish in ways you can't yet imagine."

Emily took the pouch, her heart filling with gratitude and wonder. "Thank you," she said, knowing that the enchanted seeds were a gift that would help her protect the garden and the community's heritage. "May I ask your name?"

The woman smiled warmly. "Some call me The Seed Keeper, though I'm merely a servant of the soil and the seasons. Remember, the magic of the garden is not just in the plants but in the people who care for it. You have a strong heart, Emily. Trust in yourself, and the magic will follow."

She tucked the enchanted seeds safely in her pocket, then turned to leave the market with renewed determination. The woman's words ran through her thoughts. *Use them with care.* Wondering if there was a special place she should plant them, she turned to ask, but the woman was gone. The twinkling lights and ivy decorations were gone. All that remained was a simple wooden booth.

The booth that had appeared so full of life and magic only moments before was now nothing more than an unremarkable wooden structure blending into the background of the bustling market. Heart pounding, she reached into her pocket, touching the small pouch of seeds, their presence solid and real against her fingertips.

A shiver ran down her spine—not of fear, but of awe. The encounter was like a dream, yet the weight of the seeds in her pocket assured her it was not. She glanced around, hoping to catch another glimpse of the kindly woman, but the market continued its lively hum as if nothing unusual had transpired.

With a deep breath, Emily turned and made her way back toward the path that would lead her home. The world around her seemed to pulse with a quiet energy, a reminder of the magic that lingered in the corners of Blue Ridge Haven. The woman's parting words echoed in her mind: *Trust in yourself, and the magic will follow.*

As she walked, Emily couldn't help but think the seeds were more than just a gift. They were a responsibility, a reminder of the legacy she was now a part of. Her grandmother had always believed in the unseen forces that nurtured the land, and now the belief had been passed down to her.

The path shimmered once more as she left the market square, but this time, it didn't lead her anywhere new. It simply guided her back to where she had started, back to the farmhouse and the garden that awaited her care. She smiled to herself, a sense of purpose settling in her heart.

She knew, with a certainty that went beyond reason, that these seeds would play a crucial role in the garden's restoration. But she also knew that the true magic lay not just in the seeds but in the love and dedication she would pour into the soil. The garden, like her life, was ready to bloom anew.

With the seeds safely tucked in her pocket and a heart full of renewed determination, Emily was ready to face whatever challenges lay ahead. The journey was just beginning, and she had a feeling that Blue Ridge Haven had many more secrets to reveal.

13

GATHERING STORMS

In the soft twilight of a Blue Ridge Haven evening, Emily found herself seated across from Maggie and Alex on the rustic porch of the old farmhouse. The air was thick with the scent of blooming jasmine. The garden lay before them, a testament to their progress, yet Emily's heart was heavy with the news she had to share.

"I learned something concerning at the yoga studio this morning," she said, her voice tinged with worry. "The Henderson property next door might be sold soon...to developers."

Maggie's expression turned solemn. "Developers?" she echoed, the weight of the word hanging in the air. "I've heard rumors of it being sold, but to developers?"

Alex leaned forward, his usual calm demeanor giving way to concern. "That could change everything," he said. "For the entire community."

Just then, the sound of footsteps approached the porch, and a familiar figure emerged from the twilight.

"Liam," Emily greeted him, a note of relief in her voice. "You've heard about the developers?"

Liam's face was set in a grim line. "Yes, and I've been talking to some folks. There's a lot of concern out there. This isn't just about our garden. It's about the entire area."

Emily nodded, a knot of anxiety in her stomach. "Susan and June, the women I met, they mentioned it could lead to major construction. It's not just the view that would change; it's the entire character of this neighborhood."

Maggie sighed, a look of resolve crossing her face. "We can't let that happen. Cora's garden is a piece of Blue Ridge Haven's history, a piece of our community's soul."

Ever the pragmatist, Alex chimed in, "We need to find out more about these developers, their plans, and how far along they are with their negotiations. There might be a way to challenge the development or at least influence it to be more in harmony with the community. Liam, with your experience, maybe you could help us understand our options?"

"Absolutely," Liam agreed. "Environmental impact assessments, community engagement. These are all angles we can explore."

Emily recognized a spark of hope amid the concern. Her grandmother would have fought with everything she could. Emily couldn't let her down. "What if we organized a community meeting? Get the neighbors, local businesses, anyone who cares about preserving the essence of this area. We could raise awareness, even gather support to petition against the development. We could create a group on social media so we can all stay up-to-date and organize meetings. Liam, could you help spearhead this with me?"

"Of course," he replied. "This garden has brought us together. Perhaps it can unite the community, too. I'll start reaching out to my contacts, see what I can dig up about the developers and any potential legal angles we might have."

Maggie's eyes lit up. "That's a brilliant idea, Emily."

"June and Susan mentioned the local market. They said I could probably find some allies there. They said I could meet the heart and soul of Blue Ridge Haven. I stopped there before I came home today and met so many amazing people. I think I'll go back tomorrow."

"I could go with you. I love the local market. I haven't been in a while. It would be a nice outing," Maggie said. "That is, if you don't mind me tagging along."

"I don't mind at all." Emily smiled.

"Well, it's time I refreshed my memory." Maggie patted her leg.

Emily shared her concerns about the Henderson property and the potential threat of development. Approaching footsteps suddenly cut the soft evening air. They turned to see a figure emerging from the twilight, his presence almost startling in the evening's quiet.

The man who approached was tall, his silhouette outlined against the fading light. He moved with a confident stride, his posture conveying an air of purpose. As he stepped into the soft glow of the porch light, his features became clear. He was in his mid-thirties, with dark chestnut hair that was short, giving him a neat, professional appearance. His hazel eyes, sharp and assessing, scanned the group before settling on Emily with an intensity that revealed itself as both invasive and curious. His skin bore the light tan of someone who spent time outdoors, yet there was a certain city polish about him. His attire was a blend of business and practicality —clearly out of place in the rustic setting of the farmhouse and garden.

"Good evening. I hope I'm not intruding," he began, his voice carrying a smooth confidence that hinted at many such conversations, perhaps in boardrooms or negotiations. "My name is Oliver Marshall. I represent the developers interested in the Henderson property."

Before he could come closer, Liam quietly stepped up to survey the newcomer with a steady, direct gaze. There was an immediate tension in the air, a silent clash of energies as the two men regarded each other.

Maggie, Alex, and Emily exchanged wary glances. Oliver's arrival embodied the looming threat they'd just been discussing. Liam certainly noticed, there was something about his demeanor that suggested he hadn't arrived for a confrontation.

Oliver stepped forward. "I heard and understand your concerns," he began, his voice calm and assured. "And I'm here to listen, maybe even to find a path forward that will respect both your connections to this land and the potential for its future."

His proposal to discuss their concerns was unexpected, and despite their initial mistrust, Emily found herself intrigued, not just by his words but by the contradiction he presented. Here was a man, clearly molded by the world of development and progress, standing amid the garden they were fighting to protect, offering dialogue instead of dictation.

Oliver's gaze swept over the garden, which was visible from the porch. A flash of genuine appreciation flickered in his eyes. It was only a moment, easily missed, but it spoke to a depth beyond the developer's façade. Perhaps, Emily thought, there was more to Oliver Marshall than the imminent threat he represented.

Maggie's eyes narrowed slightly, her stance firm. "Our primary concern is preserving this garden and the heritage it represents. Can your development plans accommodate that?" she asked, her voice tinged with skepticism.

Oliver nodded, acknowledging the challenge. "I believe there's always room for compromise. But first, I'd like to understand why this place is so special to you all."

Liam studied Oliver, his posture tense but controlled. "Words and promises are one thing," he said, seeming to choose each word carefully. "The actions that follow will determine the true cost." For a moment, their gazes locked, and an unspoken challenge passed between them. Aware of the tension, Emily interpreted their intensity as mere professional rivalry.

"Let's keep this civil," she intervened, her voice steady. "There's too much at stake to let emotions cloud our judgment."

Oliver turned to her, his demeanor instantly polite. "Of course. I look forward to further discussions."

Playing peacekeeper, Alex suggested, "Let's show him around. Words can't capture the essence of this place." The group agreed, and together they descended the porch steps, their figures blending into the garden's tapestry of shadows and moonlight.

Emily shared stories of her grandmother Cora as they walked, the garden's origins, and its role as a sanctuary for those seeking solace and connection. Liam shared the meaning of each of the plants they encountered. The surrounding air seemed to shimmer with a faint glow, a subtle sign that the garden itself was listening, sensing the presence of strangers.

Oliver listened intently, his gaze sweeping over the lush greenery, the vibrant patches of flowers, and the weathered stones marking hidden paths. He paused at the heart of the garden, under the ancient oak that had witnessed countless seasons. "I see why this place matters to you," he admitted, his voice softer now. "It's more than just land. It's a legacy of care, growth, and community."

As if sensing an opportunity to confront Oliver, Liam stepped closer, his voice edged with suspicion. "Legacy and community don't seem to fit into your usual plans. Why the sudden change of heart?"

Oliver met Liam's gaze evenly, a faint smirk playing on his lips. "Because even I can see the value in preserving something as cherished as this garden. It's not about destroying it. It's about integrating it into a greater vision."

Turning to face the group, Oliver took a deep breath before presenting his proposal. "What if the development included a dedicated space for this garden? A community park, perhaps, preserving Cora's legacy while integrating it into something beneficial for the entire community."

Maggie crossed her arms, considering the proposal, while Liam listened intently, and Alex looked thoughtfully at the ground. Hope mingled with uncertainty and washed through Emily. Could a compromise truly preserve what mattered most about the garden?

Liam's skepticism was noticeable. "And how do we know this isn't just a ploy? A way to gain our trust before tearing down what we hold dear?"

Oliver's expression hardened, his voice dropping to a steely tone. "I'm offering a solution that benefits everyone. It's more than I have to do, given the legal standing of the development. You can either work with me or fight a battle you're destined to lose."

The night air grew cooler as they returned to the porch. The conversation now centered on possibilities, challenges, and what compromise might mean for the future. Oliver's unexpected proposal had opened the door to dialogue, but the path forward remained uncertain.

Oliver departed, promising to return with more concrete plans. The group sat in silence, pondering the garden's fate. Emily gazed at the moonlit paths winding through the garden, symbolizing the journeys yet to come. The night ended with a sense of cautious optimism, a shared understanding that the fight for the garden—and for what it represented—was far from over.

The group dispersed, but Emily remained on the porch for a while longer, the surrounding garden bathed in the silvery light of the moon. She could hear the faint, melodic whispers of the garden fairies, their presence a comforting reminder of the magic within the soil and plants. Their gentle glow illuminated the path ahead, hinting at the hidden strength and unity that could help them overcome the challenges to come.

With a newfound sense of resolve, Emily whispered a quiet promise to the garden and to her grandmother's memory. "We will protect this place. Together, we'll keep its magic alive."

14

A DAY AT THE MARKET

The local market was a bustling hub of artisans, farmers, and craftspeople. The air was filled with the lively chatter of vendors and the tantalizing aromas of fresh food and flowers. Overhead, a flock of iridescent butterflies danced in the sunlight, their wings shimmering with colors that seemed almost magical.

Emily and Maggie wandered through the stalls, admiring handcrafted jewelry, vintage clothing, and organic produce. Emily's attention was drawn to a booth adorned with vibrant paintings. Liam was deeply engaged in conversation with the artist, his interest in local culture evident in his enthusiastic gestures.

"Hello, Liam," Emily acknowledged him.

"Hello, ladies. What brings you here?"

"Emily and I are refreshing our memory of the market." Maggie smiled.

Behind the booth stood a young woman, her sandy blonde hair in a loose braid adorned with a small, colorful flower. Her eclectic style, a mix of bohemian and vintage, mirrored her artistic spirit, and her gentle demeanor set her apart. As Emily and Maggie approached the booth, Emily couldn't help but be drawn in by the artwork's depth and color. "These are beautiful," she exclaimed, picking up a canvas depicting the Blue Ridge Mountains bathed in sunlight.

"Thank you," the young woman replied with a smile. "I'm Maya Carter. My own experiences and the beauty of Blue Ridge Haven inspired each piece."

Maggie, curious about the people in her community, said, "Your booth adds a lot to the market, Maya."

Maya's thoughtful eyes, reflecting a wisdom beyond her years, lingered on her paintings before meeting theirs. "Do you see anything you like? I can tell you about why I painted it."

"Maya's work really captures the spirit of Blue Ridge Haven, don't you think?" Liam turned, his face lighting up.

"I agree with Liam. Your work speaks volumes. What inspires you?" Maggie asked.

Maya hesitated, her gaze falling briefly on her slightly rounded belly before returning to her air. "Life's been...a little unexpected lately," she said, glancing at her paintings. "I'm just trying to figure things out, like everyone else."

There was a pause, a silent acknowledgment of shared vulnerabilities. A faint glow seemed to emanate from the paintings, and Emily thought she saw a fleeting image of a fairy dancing in the background of one piece, only to disappear when she blinked.

"I'm pregnant. It wasn't part of the plan, but...here I am," she said, smiling a little sadly. "Just me and my paints, figuring it out."

Emily listened to Maya's hesitancy and eventual sharing about her pregnancy. Her heart swelled with a mix of emotions. There was an instant connection. Her own pain and longing for motherhood, the absence of a spouse echoing in Maya's story. This encounter stirred a deep empathy within her, mingling with admiration for Maya's resilience. Emily's journey with the garden had been one of seeking healing and purpose, and now, standing before Maya, she saw a reflection of her own struggles, but also of hope and the possibility of new beginnings. Emily shared softly, "We all have our gardens to tend, literal or metaphorical. I'm here trying to breathe new life into my grandmother's garden and, in a way, into myself."

Always the nurturer, Maggie suggested, "Why don't we join forces? Your art could inspire not just us but the community. The garden could serve as a sanctuary for all kinds of growth. Maybe you could sell some of your paintings in the garden."

"I'd like that," Maya said, a smile breaking through her initial reservation. "I think I'd like that very much."

"I could help you navigate the logistical aspects of integrating your art into community spaces," Liam offered. "I have connections with potential venues where you could showcase your work."

"I would appreciate any help you could give me. Thank you, Liam." Maya smiled.

"Where do you live, Maya?" Emily asked. "I'd love to keep in touch and maybe visit your studio sometime."

She hesitated, her eyes reflecting a mix of pride and vulnerability. "I actually don't have a studio. I carry all my supplies in my van."

"You don't have a room to paint wherever you live?" Emily prodded.

"I'm living out of my van. I've struggled to find stable housing. One reason I'm here selling my paintings is to hopefully save enough money to find a place." Maya didn't make eye contact.

"What about your family?" Liam asked.

"They are emotionally supportive. Unfortunately, they don't have the resources to be financially supportive. Besides, I want to provide a secure future for my child. I'm taking fine arts classes at the community college," Maya explained.

Emily continued to listen to Maya's story as a whirlwind of emotions churned within her. She noticed an unexpected kinship, a shared understanding of facing life's unpredictability. "I have plenty of room at my farmhouse," she said, the words almost surprising her. As she spoke, a part of her wondered about the implications of inviting a stranger into her life. Yet another part said this was exactly what her grandmother's legacy inspired. Acts of kindness and community.

Maya's hesitation was noticeable, her pride wrestling with her need. Emily could see the struggle in her eyes, the desire for a haven clashing with the fear of accepting help. "I...couldn't," she murmured, but Emily saw the slight falter, the silent plea for something stable.

"Please, won't you consider it?" Emily pressed gently, her voice quietly insistent. She thought of her own journey, the solitude of the garden, and how much richer the experience could be with shared purpose. "Maggie lives right next door. I hate to think about you in your condition, living out of a van."

This wasn't just about offering Maya a room. It was about weaving new threads into the fabric of their lives, creating a tapestry of support, growth, and perhaps healing. Finally, Maya nodded, a silent agreement passing between them, and a warmth spread through Emily. This was more than an act of kindness. It was a step toward fulfilling a legacy of love, connection, and renewal that her grandmother had left behind.

"You could put her to work in the garden," Maggie interjected. "That is, if Maya feels she can't stay with you and not pay for her room. If she sells her paintings there, she could pay you something out of her sales."

"That's a great idea. What about it, Maya? I would love to have you." Emily's eyes reflected the sincerity she was offering.

"It would be a great setup," Liam added.

"Are you sure about this?" Maya asked.

"I'm positive. Here's my address." Emily scribbled the address of the farmhouse on a flyer lying on the table. "Stop by when you're finished here and I'll show you the rooms. You can pick the one that is most comfortable." Her posture straightened. If she couldn't bring life into this world, she would at least do what she could to help other women who were lucky enough to experience motherhood.

After saying their goodbyes to Liam, Emily and Maggie left the market. Emily sensed a kinship with Maya. "Today was about more than just finding beautiful art. It was about finding strength in our stories."

Maggie agreed, "It's the unexpected encounters that often lead to the most beautiful gardens."

The idea of joining forces with Maya not only excited Emily but also infused her project with a deeper meaning. It wasn't just about reviving a garden anymore; it was about nurturing life in all its forms and creating a space where healing and growth could flourish. Her commitment to the garden and to forming this new bond was now fueled by a profound sense of kinship and shared destiny.

15

BLOOMING FRIENDSHIPS

A flutter of anticipation stirred within Emily as she opened the front door to welcome Maya. Watching the young woman step over the threshold, Emily sensed hope mingling with nostalgia. The house, steeped in memories, now seemed to hold the promise of new beginnings. A soft glow seemed to emanate from the walls at Maya's entry. A warm welcome from the house itself. "Welcome. Come in," she said, her voice laced with warmth. "Let me show you around and see what you think."

"It already feels more like home than anywhere else I've been lately," Maya admitted, her voice tinged with a vulnerability that mirrored Emily's own. The flowers in Maya's hair shimmered, casting tiny sparkles of light that danced around the room.

Emily continued to lead her through the house. "Living in a van must be incredibly tough." Empathy shaded her words as they moved from space to space.

"It's taught me resilience," Maya responded, a soft strength in her voice. "But I've longed for a place to call home."

"Can I get you something to drink? I was going to make some tea and sit out on the porch," Emily said.

"I would love some. I would also like to see this garden you and

Maggie were talking about. I've heard so much about it from people in town. How you're restoring it."

"Sure. Let me show you the rooms first, then we can take our tea out on the porch. It's a beautiful evening." Emily headed up the stairs, stopping at the first bedroom. "This was always what Grandmother Cora called the guest bedroom. It was only occupied when her friends or my parents would visit."

They continued down the hallway. "The next room is the room I always stayed in when I visited."

"Are you staying in there now that your grandmother is gone?" Maya asked.

"I was, but now I'm sleeping in her room. I wanted to be close to her."

"I can understand that." Maya nodded.

"You can choose either of the other two rooms. I'll leave it up to you." Emily headed toward the stairs. "How about that tea? We can talk out on the porch."

Showing Maya the rooms, a pang of vulnerability overcame her, opening her grandmother's sanctuary to someone new. Yet, there was also a comforting sense of continuity. The house's legacy of care and refuge was being honored. Emily noticed the faint scent of lavender filling the air as they walked. A scent she remembered from her grandmother's homemade potpourri that she suspected might have been enchanted to soothe the calm.

Emily handed Maya her tea and opened the door leading out to the porch.

Maya walked out and Emily could swear she heard an audible gasp. Fireflies, brighter and more numerous than usual, illuminated the garden in a soft, magical glow.

"I've heard so much about this garden," Maya said, her gaze wandering over the lush greenery that bore the marks of Emily and her friends' recent labors. "It's even more beautiful than I imagined. I would love to help you restore it."

"You should see it in its glory. Maggie, Alex, and I are just getting it to look alive again. We'd be happy to have the help." Emily took a sip of her tea.

"There it is again," she said softly, setting her glass down.

Maya followed her line of sight, noticing the wicker basket for the first time. A sprig of rosemary tied with twine was slightly wilted from the morning dew. Inside, as always, were seed packets nestled snugly in folds of burlap.

"What is it?" Maya asked, curious.

Emily walked over to the basket, crouching beside it. "I leave this basket empty on the porch at night, and by morning, it's filled with seeds." She picked up one packet, turning it over to reveal today's words, written in the same looping, elegant script. *Endurance, Compassion, Bloom, and Patience*. The letters curled and flourished like vines, delicate yet purposeful, just like the writing on the *Enchanted Seeds and Magical Plants* sign at the market.

Maya knelt beside her, her brows lifting in amazement. "And you have no idea who's leaving them?"

"I met an older woman at the market," Emily explained, her voice quiet, as though speaking too loudly might break the spell. "She said she was The Seed Keeper. I smelled the same scent of cedar and citrus blossoms at her booth that I smell on these seeds. I'm not sure. It's the only clue I have."

Maya's fingers brushed one packet labeled *Compassion*. She smiled faintly. "It's almost like the garden itself is finding a way to reach out to you. Like it knows you need these seeds to thrive."

Emily's heart swelled at the thought. Her gaze drifted toward the sprawling garden, where blooms trembled softly in the breeze. "Maybe it does. Or maybe someone in this town knows how much this place means and wants to see it thrive again." She smiled, her fingers curling gently around the basket's handle. "I can show you around the garden or we can sit and talk. I assume you've had a long day on your feet."

Maya placed a hand on her back as she arched. "It's amazing how much the small amount of weight I've gained can make my back hurt." She sat down in the empty chair. As she did, the garden seemed to respond to her presence. Flowers subtly turned toward her as if welcoming her.

"We'll have plenty of time for you to take a tour of the garden. Right now, you need to put your feet up and relax." Emily's heart ached with envy as she glanced at Maya's slight bump, a stark reminder of her own unfulfilled desires. Yet the envy was tempered by a growing resolve to foster a space where new life—both botanical and human—could flourish against the odds.

"Which side of the garden is the one you and Maggie were saying the development company wants to buy?" Maya asked.

"That side." Emily pointed toward the Henderson property. "I guess they're trying to buy the land from the Hendersons. I'm not sure exactly what they plan to do, but two women in yoga class told me it was trouble."

"Trouble?" Maya asked.

"That's the same thing I asked. All they said was it would be a significant threat to the community's character. Everyone I've talked to seems to love this community the way it is. They're all against significant change. It's a quiet, peaceful, safe neighborhood. I would hate to see the development company come in and create chaos. I need to do more research to find out what it is they are planning."

"I'll be happy to keep my ears open while I'm at the art festival. People love to talk about community issues," Maya offered.

"Thank you. I would appreciate that."

"Can I ask you something?" Maya glanced at Emily.

"Sure. Ask away."

"When I met you and Maggie today, you said you were navigating some personal challenges and were trying to find your footing."

Emily nodded.

"Can I ask what those challenges are? You seemed understanding when I told you about my pregnancy and the father not wanting to be involved."

"Of course." Emily paused. "My husband and I are having problems, and yesterday I received the divorce papers he filed."

"I'm so sorry," Maya interrupted.

"Thanks. We've been trying to have a baby for the past several years. I learned I'm not able to. My husband believes we put all our attention on having a baby and that we lost touch with each other. We became just the means to an end instead of a couple."

"Do you believe that too?" Maya asked.

"I don't know what I believe anymore. That's one reason I came here. I needed time away. I guess Mark decided he needed time away for good."

"It's probably hard for you to see me in the situation I'm in when you tried so hard to have a baby of your own."

Emily could only smile. Instead of answering, she looked out into the garden, bathed in the evening light. A sense of peace rushed over her. This unexpected journey that brought Maya into her life was a serendipitous twist of fate that could lead to healing for them both. The connection to her grandmother's legacy felt more intense than it had been since she arrived. The garden's restoration and Maya's presence symbolized new beginnings and the potential for growth and healing.

A faint silvery mist rose from the ground as they sat in the tranquil garden. It swirled gently around the plants and flowers, making the garden look like a scene from a fairy tale. Tiny, glowing orbs—like miniature stars—floated within the mist, casting a magical light over everything.

Wide-eyed, Maya watched in awe. "What is that?" she whispered.

Emily smiled. Her heart was full. "It's the garden's way of welcoming you," she said. "This place has always had a bit of magic. My grandmother used to say that the garden responds to those who need it the most."

The mist swirled around them as they talked, bringing with it a sense of calm and wonder. The garden, with its hidden magic and promise of renewal, was the perfect place for both Emily and Maya to find the healing and new beginnings they so desperately sought.

16

NEW BEGINNINGS, SHARED JOURNEYS

In the crisp morning air, Emily set out for the garden, her basket filled with new seeds that had replenished the ones planted yesterday. Her heart was heavy with thoughts. Intending to breathe life into a neglected corner, she planted the variety of seeds —lavender, chamomile, and wildflowers, hoping to see them sprout in the coming weeks. Her next chore would be tending to a particularly stubborn rose bush. An inexplicable intuition guided her to plant a collection of flowers that didn't belong to the native flora of Blue Ridge Haven. Trusting the guidance of the whispers and the seed fairy, she planted in the designated spots, curiosity and wonder stirring in her heart. As she pressed them into the soil, a faint, shimmering light seemed to linger around her fingertips, hinting at the magic within the seeds.

Hearing a noise behind her, she looked up to see Maggie approaching. A small, gentle breeze ruffled the leaves as if the garden itself welcomed her.

"Good morning, Maggie. You're here early," Emily remarked, a gentle smile playing on her lips. She was grateful for the sight of a friend.

Maggie returned her smile, her gaze drifting momentarily to the basket of seeds on the porch. She lifted the basket slightly. "How did it go with Maya? Did she decide to stay with you or continue living out of her van?"

Emily hesitated, unsure how Maggie felt about the situation. The decision to invite Maya to stay had been spontaneous, driven by empathy and a desire to help. "Yes. She decided she would stay."

Maggie's eyebrow rose in surprise, but her expression softened into one of understanding. "I'm glad you offered her a place to stay."

"Me, too," Emily confirmed, brushing a strand of hair from her face. "She's going through a rough patch, and this place...it's big, Maggie. Too big for just me. I remembered what Grandmother always said about the house being a haven for those in need. It just felt right."

Maggie nodded, setting the basket down on the porch step. "Cora would be proud," she said, her voice imbued with warmth. "And I'm proud of you, Emily. It takes a big heart to open up your home like that."

There was a pause, a comfortable silence that spoke volumes of their friendship. "Thank you, Maggie. That means a lot to me."

"Is Maya here?" Maggie asked. "I would like to say hello to her."

"She was up and gone early this morning. She wanted to set up her space at the local market," Emily explained.

"Well, I'll just have to talk to her another time. Right now, put me to work. Where do you want me to plant these seeds?" Maggie picked up the basket again.

"Wherever you think they would look beautiful. I trust your instinct for the garden." Emily smiled as she watched Maggie select a plot of dirt and start digging into the soil. The ground seemed to respond, small tendrils of roots reaching out eagerly as if craving her touch. Maggie's unwavering support for weaving Maya into the fabric of their lives was important and a surge of gratitude went through Emily. They were creating a new chapter in the garden's story, one that promised growth, healing, and new beginnings.

"What if we visit Maya at her booth? We can have lunch there," Emily suggested.

"I would like that," Maggie said, as she continued planting seedlings. "Have you discovered who is leaving the seeds?"

"No, I haven't. I hope to catch them one of these days." Emily was just as curious as Maggie seemed to be.

"You ladies are already hard at it this morning." Alex's voice came from behind them.

"Hello, Alex," Maggie greeted him. "Grab some seeds."

"I came by to see if I could help today. I have a light schedule," Alex said.

"We can always use help." Emily shaded her eyes as she glanced at him. "There are some more seeds on the porch. Like I told Maggie, find a spot and start planting. Wherever you think it needs them."

"Emily has some news, Alex. She has a roommate," Maggie said.

His eyebrows rose in surprise. "Oh? That was unexpected. Who is it?"

"A young artist named Maya Carter. She's been living out of her van, struggling a bit. It felt right to offer her a place here," Emily explained with a hint of pride in her voice.

Alex leaned on his shovel, processing the news. "That's very generous of you, Emily. This place has always been a safe place of sorts. Sounds like Maya could use a bit of that."

"I hope so," Emily sighed, her gaze drifting to the garden's edge where shadows mingled. "It's what my grandmother would have wanted, I think. To offer shelter, to nurture not just plants but also people."

He nodded, a thoughtful look crossing his face. "You're doing a good thing, Emily. And who knows, Maya's art might add an extra dimension to this garden of yours. Healing comes in many forms."

A warmth spread through her at his words, a reassurance that she had made the right decision. "Thank you, Alex. That means a lot to me. I just want this place to be what my grandmother envisioned—a haven for those in need."

"As it should be," he agreed, offering her a supportive smile. "And if you need help with anything—fixing up a room for Maya or more hands in the garden—you know where to find me."

"I know," Emily replied, her heart lighter than it had been all day. "Thank you. Also, Maggie and I are going to have lunch at the market. You're welcome to join us."

"I would like that." Alex smiled.

He went back to his work and Emily to hers. The garden seemed to hum with a silent approval. The decision to open her home to Maya, to extend the sanctuary her grandmother had created, was the first step toward a future she hadn't dared to envision. One filled with new friendships, healing, and the magical intertwining of lives.

The air at the local market was vibrant, filled with chatter of vendors and the mingling aromas of fresh produce and baked goods. Emily, Maggie, and Alex navigated through the bustling stalls, each step bringing a new discovery. Today was special. Emily was eager to introduce Alex to Maya, whose presence had already woven new patterns into the fabric of Emily's life.

They settled down at a small eatery known for its organic delicacies and rustic charm. Emily's gaze caught a familiar figure threading through the crowd. It was Oliver Marshall, his casual yet purposeful stride unmistakable even from a distance.

Spotting the group, Oliver's face lit up with a warm smile, and he made his way over. "Fancy meeting you all here," he said, his voice carrying a genuine note of happiness at the chance encounter.

"We're here to enjoy some of the market's best offerings and to catch up with a friend," Emily explained, her tone inviting. "Would you like to join us? There's plenty of room."

Oliver glanced at their table's inviting array of dishes, then back to the group. "I'd love to, if you don't mind. It's a perfect day to share good food and company."

"Maya should join us soon," Emily said to Alex, her voice tinged with excitement. "I think you'll like her. She's an artist with a spirit as nurturing as her art."

An unmistakable air of warmth floated around Maya as she approached. Her smile, bright and genuine, bridged any gaps of unfamiliarity. Emily stood up when she arrived, gesturing toward Alex and Oliver.

"Maya, this is Alex. Alex, Maya is the roommate I was telling you about," Emily introduced them.

"It's a pleasure to meet you," Alex said, extending his hand in greeting. "Emily's told us a lot about you and your art. It sounds like you're bringing a new life to the garden and the farmhouse."

Maya's cheeks colored slightly at the compliment. "Thank you, Alex. I've heard about your contributions, too. It seems we're all part of this garden's new chapter."

Emily motioned to Oliver. "And this is Oliver Marshall. We met him last night. The development company who wants to purchase the Henderson property employs him."

Oliver stood and extended his hand for Maya to shake. "I've also heard a lot about your art. I can't wait to see it."

"I'll be happy to show you some after lunch," Maya offered.

The conversation flowed easily, as if they were old friends. Maggie shared stories of the garden's past glories while Alex spoke of his plans to help restore it. Maya listened intently, occasionally sharing her own visions of how art could intertwine with nature to create a sanctuary not just for them but for the entire community.

Oliver explained about exploring sustainable initiatives to develop the Henderson property. "We're trying to find a balance that respects the community and the environment," he said. His earnest tone reflected his evolving perspective, influenced by his interactions with the garden.

The bond between them deepened as they ate, and each story and shared laugh added layers to their burgeoning friendship. Emily watched her new friends come together, contentment settling over her. The garden had brought them all here, binding their lives in unexpected, beautiful ways. Small motes of light, almost like fairy lights, twinkled above their table, unnoticed by most but adding a magical glow to their gathering.

Walking back through the market, Emily reflected on the unexpected journey that had brought them all together. Oliver's involvement had strengthened from a potential adversary to a collaborative partner, illustrating the transformative power of open dialogue and shared visions for the future.

The laughter and chatter around her ebbed and flowed. Emily's thoughts momentarily drifted to Liam. He was the only person missing from the group. With his deep understanding of nature and its rhythms, he always had a way of grounding her. His presence brought a calm to the bustling energy of community gatherings. Unless Oliver was around. The tension between the two of them was palpable.

She missed the thoughtful tilt of his head when Liam listened, the way his eyes lit up when he spoke about the Blue Ridge Haven landscape or the gentle authority with which he guided their environmental efforts. Today, amid the colorful chaos of the market and the warmth of new connections, there was a pang of longing for his steady companionship.

It was Liam's unique perspective on the natural world, his commitment to preserving its beauty, that often inspired her. He had a way of seeing beyond the immediate. A vision that stretched into the roots and soul of the land. Without him, the day seemed slightly less complete, a reminder of how much his presence enriched her life.

Sighing softly, Emily glanced around, half-expecting to see him walking toward them with a smile, ready to share a discovery or a new idea that would benefit their community project. Moments like this underscored how integral Liam had become, not only to the project but to her personal circle. His absence was acutely noticeable amid the collective joy of shared goals.

She made a mental note to reach out to him later, hoping to share the day's experiences and maybe coax him back into the fold for the next gathering. After all, their garden and their lives seemed more vibrant with Liam's involvement, his spirit a crucial thread woven into the fabric of their community.

17

A MEAL TO REMEMBER

The sun set as Emily finished working. Maya stood nearby, tending to the last of the wildflowers they'd planted that afternoon. The golden hour illuminated the blooms and the farmhouse with a soft light. A familiar voice came from behind them.

"Hard at work, I see," Liam said, approaching with a smile. "How about you call it a day and we have dinner together?"

Emily brushed her hair back and stood up, curious. "Dinner? What did you have in mind?"

"A little surprise," Liam replied, his eyes twinkling. "Something special for all the hard work you've both been putting in. I'll handle everything. You two just relax."

"You mean you're cooking?" Maya asked, her eyes sparkling.

"Of course." Liam smiled. "That is if Emily will allow me to use her kitchen."

"I'm in," Maya laughed and turned to Emily. "What about you?"

With a brief hesitation, Emily answered, "Sure. That sounds good."

Inside the farmhouse, the aromatic scent of sautéing garlic and herbs was in the air. Maya sat at the kitchen table, watching Liam move through the kitchen with ease while Emily lit a few candles to add to the cozy atmosphere.

Liam unpacked a bag of groceries and explained, "I used to make a mean chicken marsala. I thought tonight would be a good night to bring that back."

Emily's breath caught as she looked at the ingredients on the counter. The memory of Mark in their kitchen, carefully preparing the same dish, flashed before her eyes. "Mark loves to make that dish," she whispered. "And he was good at it, too."

Liam nodded with a knowing smile, and the meal unfolded beautifully. The three of them chatted lightly while the chicken simmered, creating a fragrant sauce that reminded Emily of those long-ago evenings. She helped Liam with the plating and set out simple, elegant servings on the table.

They laughed and shared stories while eating. The garden outside shimmered with a soft, ethereal light. Tiny luminescent fairies emerged from the flowers, their delicate wings glistening like dew in the morning. They danced and flitted about, casting a magical ambiance over the evening.

"Look at that," Maya whispered, pointing to the fairies. "I've heard stories about the garden's magic, but I never believed it until now."

Emily smiled, her heart warming at the sight. "My grandmother used to tell me tales of the garden's enchantments. She said the fairies appear to bless moments of true happiness."

She stood at the sink after dinner, rinsing the dishes. Liam came up beside her, quietly picking up a towel to dry them. For a moment, there was silence, then Liam spoke up gently. "How are you feeling?"

She glanced at him thoughtfully. "It's hard to explain," she admitted. "This meal brought back so many memories. I appreciate you making it for us."

Liam nodded. "When you mentioned Mark made this dish, I thought it might help you remember how special those memories are."

"Those are memories I've been trying to not remember." Emily wiped her hands on the dish towel and turned to face Liam. "I'm grateful for your support," she said. "And for being such a good friend to me and Maya."

He smiled warmly. "Friends look out for each other."

Maya spoke up as they finished clearing away the dishes, "I'm exhausted. I hope you don't think I'm being rude if I go to my room and rest?"

"No, not at all. Go ahead. We're almost done here," Emily said.

"Thank you so much for dinner, Liam. It was so delicious. I'm going to have to learn your recipe." Maya waved as she disappeared up the stairs.

"You're welcome," Liam said. "Well, I believe it's time for me to leave."

"It was so nice of you to think of Maya and me." Emily hung the dish towel over the oven handle to dry. Her fondness for Liam was outweighed by the bittersweet nostalgia conjured up by the meal he'd prepared. She enjoyed Liam's company, but the pain of her and Mark's divorce hadn't fully healed.

"I was happy to." Liam smiled. "If you're alright, I'm going to leave now. Let you get some rest." Liam gave her a hug. "I'm just a phone call away if you need anything."

Emily watched as he walked out the front door of the farmhouse. She was alone with her thoughts and feelings. Her inner turmoil left her questioning the path forward. She needed clarity in the tangle of emotions she was having.

She lingered for a moment in the dimly lit kitchen, and the remaining aroma of dinner mingled with the warm memories the evening had stirred up. She sighed softly, extinguishing the candles one by one before heading upstairs to her bedroom.

The old farmhouse creaked gently under her steps as she moved down the hallway. Her room was filled with comforting shadows that wrapped around her like a warm blanket. Her eyes drifted to Rosie, still in her place on the pillow. She settled herself at the small writing desk in the corner, opened her journal, and picked up her favorite pen.

The first few words came easily, but soon, she stared at the page, lost in thought. Liam's kindness tugged at her heart, and she couldn't deny the sense of warmth and safety when she was around him. But each gesture he made, thoughtful and gentle, was a ghostly echo of Mark.

The day at the market and his encouraging words had also reminded her of moments she shared with Mark during the best days of their marriage.

She tapped the pen against her lips and wrote slowly: *Liam's kindness reminds me of Mark's caring ways. Tonight's dinner brought back so many memories. It was almost like Mark was here.*

But then she paused. Her heart ached at the thought. Despite the tenderness she had experienced during dinner, she recognized that her love for Mark still ran deep, even if the reality of their marriage had grown complicated. The divorce papers were real, but the feelings weren't so easily cut off.

Her eyes drifted over to an old photo sitting on the shelf. She hesitated for a moment before picking it up and dusting it off. It was a picture of her and Mark on one of their visits to the farmhouse. They were laughing and happy as they visited with family, arms wrapped around each other like it was them against the world.

She placed the photo back in its place, her fingers tracing the frame. Her mind replayed the best moments of their marriage. Lazy Sunday mornings with homemade breakfasts, the joy of spontaneous road trips, and the comfort of being with someone who understood her deeply. There had been pain, too, and she couldn't ignore the bitter arguments, the frustration of infertility, and the distance that had crept between them. But was it too late to rebuild?

She sighed deeply, laying her head down on the desk. She needed to understand what she wanted, to find the right path through the tangle of emotions. Was Liam's kindness and gentle support simply a balm for her wounds, or could there be something more between them? And if there was, would it ever compare to what she'd once had with Mark?

She closed her eyes, the swirl of thoughts mingling in her head as sleep slowly overtook her. The photo rested by her side, a silent reminder of the lover she'd known and the uncertain journey ahead.

Outside, the garden glowed softly under the moonlight, the fairies continuing their silent dance, casting a protective spell over Emily and the farmhouse, ensuring that whatever path she chose, she would never walk alone.

18

A DREAM OF HOPE

The night was quiet when Emily finally moved from the desk into bed. Her mind replayed the events of the day, the warmth of the dinner, and the kindness of Liam's gesture. A sense of peace engulfed her as she drifted to sleep. Rosie lay beside her on the pillow.

In her dream, Emily found herself in the middle of a lush, vibrant garden, not unlike her grandmother's. The flowers were in full bloom, their colors vivid and rich. She had an overwhelming sense of contentment and joy as she walked through the garden, touching the petals and inhaling the fragrant, enchanted air.

A small, cozy cottage at the garden's edge drew her attention, pulling her toward it like a magnet. Light filled the cottage, and the air was warm and inviting inside. She saw herself in a mirror, and to her surprise, she was pregnant. Her hands instinctively moved to her rounded belly, and she felt the baby's gentle kick. The sensation was so real, so profound, that tears of joy streamed down her face.

Mark appeared beside her, his eyes filled with love and happiness. They embraced, and an overwhelming sense of completeness filled her. The baby kicked again, and they laughed, sharing a moment of pure bliss as they stood in front of the mirror, rubbing her belly. The joy rushed through her. This was everything she and Mark always wanted. The years of infertility and pain were finally over.

Suddenly, the mirror shimmered, and the reflection changed. The garden outside the cottage was now filled with fantastical creatures—fairies with delicate wings fluttered around, unicorns grazed peacefully, and the flowers sang a gentle lullaby. The air was thick with magic. It seeped into her very being.

Emily woke with a start, the remnants of the dream clinging to her consciousness. Her hands moved to her flat stomach, and reality came crashing down. She wasn't pregnant. She had never conceived. The dream was so real, so hopeful, that waking up was a harsh reminder of her reality. As tears filled her eyes, she noticed Rosie lying beside her on the bed, her tiny face gazing at her with a serene expression.

Lying back against the pillows, she tried to shake off the lingering emotions. The dream had brought to the surface all her deepest fears and desires. The familiar ache of longing, the sorrow of her unfulfilled dreams, and the painful reminder of her struggles.

She got out of bed and wrapped herself in a robe, needing the comfort of the cool night air. From the front porch, she stared at the garden bathed in the soft glow of the moonlight. The beauty of the night seemed to mock her inner turmoil, and a deep, wrenching sadness overwhelmed her.

Emily stood there, trying to find solace in the quiet night. A soft, melodious chime echoed through the garden. She turned to see a small, sparkling creature hovering near her. It was a fairy, its wings shimmering with iridescent light.

"Welcome, Emily," the fairy said in a voice like tinkling bells. "I'm Liora, guardian of this garden. Your dreams and hopes have not gone unnoticed. The magic of this place is strong, and it responds to the deepest desires of those who tend it with love."

Emily's eyes widened with wonder. "Liora?" she whispered, barely believing what she was seeing.

Liora nodded, her presence radiating a calming energy. "Yes, Emily. We've met before, a long time ago, when you were just a child."

A memory surfaced in Emily's mind, taking her back to a night years ago when she was staying with her grandmother, Cora. She had been upset, crying over her mother's demands. Cora had taken her out to the garden, where the moonlight bathed everything in a silvery glow.

"Look, Emily," her grandmother had said, pointing to the tiny lights dancing among the flowers. "These are garden fairies. They come out when someone with a pure heart needs comfort."

Young Emily had wiped her tears, staring in awe at the delicate creatures. Slightly larger and brighter than the others, one had hovered closer to her, whispering soothing words. "I'm Liora," the fairy said. "Whenever you're sad, remember that you are never alone."

The memory faded, and Emily looked at Liora with newfound recognition. "You comforted me when I was a child," she said, her voice trembling.

Liora smiled warmly. "Yes, I also came to comfort you when you were here after your grandmother Cora went to another realm."

"You were here then?" Emily asked.

Liora nodded. "I was, but you were much older, and your heart was closed off to the possibilities, so I was unable to appear to you. I sent you love and comfort, though. I hope you felt it. All the fairies were sending you loving energy and warmth. I'm here now to remind you of the magic that still exists in this garden and within you. You have opened up to it since you've been here."

"I'm so sorry I couldn't see you. I could have used your comfort." A tear slid down Emily's cheek. "I had a dream," she confessed. "It seemed so real. I was pregnant, and Mark was there. It was everything I've ever wanted, but it was just a dream."

"Dreams can be powerful," Liora said gently. "They can show us our deepest desires and fears. But they can also be a source of hope and guidance. The magic of this garden can help you heal and guide you, but you must believe in its power and your own."

Emily nodded, her heart aching but also flickering with hope. "Thank you, Liora. I don't know how, but I will try to believe."

The tiny creature fluttered closer, her light illuminating Emily's face. "You have a strong heart, Emily. Continue to nurture this garden, and it will nurture you in return. Trust in the journey, and know that you are never alone."

With that, Liora fluttered away, leaving a trail of sparkling light that lingered in the air. Emily watched her go, sensing comfort and renewed determination. She knew the road ahead wouldn't be easy, but she also knew she had the support of her friends, the magic of the garden, and the memory of her grandmother to guide her.

The next morning, Emily was a bit more composed but still shaken from the dream. She walked outside and found the basket full of seeds and Maya in the garden, working on a new painting. The sight of the vibrant colors and Maya's focused expression brought a small smile to her face.

"Morning, Maya," she greeted her.

Maya looked up and smiled. "Morning, Emily." She gestured to the canvas. "I started working on something new. I had this vision last night, and I couldn't wait to get started."

Emily walked over, curious. Her breath caught when she saw the painting. It was a beautiful, ethereal depiction of a pregnant woman surrounded by blooming flowers. The woman's face bore an uncanny resemblance to her. It was the vision Emily saw in her dream.

"Maya, this is...incredible," she whispered, her eyes filling with tears again.

Maya contemplated the painting. "I don't know where it came from, but I had this overwhelming need to capture it. Maybe it's a sign. Maybe it's about hope and the possibility of new beginnings."

Emily nodded, her heart swelling with a mixture of emotions. "Maybe it is," she agreed softly.

Just then, a soft, melodious chime echoed through the garden. Emily and Maya turned to see a small, sparkling creature hovering near them. It was Liora, her wings shimmering with iridescent light.

Emily stepped forward and smiled. Liora fluttered her wings once before leaving Maya and Emily in silence.

"This garden...it's truly magical," Emily said, breaking the silence.

Her voice trembling with emotion. "We really can find the happiness and healing we've been seeking."

Maya nodded, her eyes shining with determination. "We will, Emily. Together, we will."

And with renewed hope and belief in magic, they continued their journey, ready to embrace whatever the future held.

19

UNEXPLAINABLE PHENOMENON

The dawn had barely broken when Emily stepped outside, her footsteps light upon the dew-kissed earth. The crisp morning air was filled with the promise of a new day and carried a sense of anticipation. With a newly filled basket of seeds left for her on the porch in one hand and a small trowel in the other, Emily approached a corner of the garden she had earmarked for today's work. The task was simple; plant new seeds, a ritual she had performed countless times. Yet, something was different this morning, as if the garden awaited her touch with bated breath.

The patches of soil before her were unremarkable, marred only by the signs of yesterday's labor. With practiced motions, Emily planted lavender and chamomile, their scents a future promise to the air. The work was meditative, with each seed a whisper of potential life and each covering of soil a gentle tucking into bed.

However, this morning, the ordinary had turned extraordinary. Where there should have been only hints of life, timid sprouts barely breaking through, there stood small but decidedly vibrant shoots, their growth inexplicably sped up. The lavender and chamomile, especially, flaunted buds that defied the constraints of time.

Stunned, Emily crouched down, her fingers hovering, then

touching the miraculous growth. Part of her mind scrambled for a logical explanation. Had she lost track of time? But no, the sun had set and risen only once. Another part, deeper, more instinctual, accepted the phenomenon with quiet joy as if such miracles were always meant to be part of the garden's essence.

Curiosity piqued by the morning's discovery, Emily pushed the boundaries of this newfound marvel. She planted a row of sunflower seeds by the garden's edge, their future faces intended to gaze upon the sun. Yet, what should have taken weeks took mere hours. By evening, the shoots greeted her, tiny sun worshippers announcing a new era for the garden.

The garden seemed to glow with a soft, ethereal light as the evening wore on. Fireflies danced in intricate patterns, weaving through the air with an almost choreographed grace. Among the flowers, small, translucent creatures, barely a few inches tall, flitted about. These were the garden sprites, beings of pure magic that tended to the plants with a delicate touch. Their wings glistened like opals in the moonlight, and their laughter was like the twinkling of tiny bells.

That night, Emily lay awake, the day's events replaying in her mind. She remembered her grandmother Cora's tales of a living garden, a garden that whispered and cared, tales Emily had relegated to the memory of fond childhood fantasy. But now, faced with the undeniable, the garden's whispers grew louder, its embrace warmer.

Before drifting to sleep, Emily reached out to Rosie, beside her on the pillow. The doll's familiar weight in her hand brought a sense of comfort and connection. Emily knew Rosie was more than just a keepsake. She was a bridge to her grandmother's wisdom and the magic of the garden.

It was in the quiet moments that followed—moments filled with whispers on the wind that sounded like words, with flowers blooming out of turn as if in response to her thoughts, with an energy that seemed to cradle her in solitude—that Emily's bond with the garden deepened. No longer just a keeper of the land, she became its confidante, its friend.

Dawn broke on another day as Emily stood holding a basket full of gifted seeds, a gentle smile gracing her lips. The garden hummed around her, alive with magic, alive with possibilities. And Emily, heart open and spirit renewed, knew she was exactly where she needed to be—home.

The garden thrived, responding to her care with displays of magic, small and large, each a testament to its vibrant spirit. Flowers that should not bloom stood proud and full. The wind carried laughter, and the earth itself seemed to pulse with life. At night, the garden became a tapestry of forming arches and bowers that glowed softly in the starlight.

In those moments, Emily realized the garden's true nature. It was not just the soil and the bloom, but the living entity, rich in magic and mystery, capable of healing the plants within its care and the souls of those who tended it. In its silent, steadfast way, the garden mirrored Emily's journey of healing and discovery, reminding her that magic was not just in the tales of old but in the here and now, in the garden's heart, and in hers.

The night enveloped the farmhouse in a peaceful silence, the kind that seemed to blanket the world in calm. Drifting into sleep, her consciousness slipped into the realm of dreams. Here, the garden was alive, not with the physical growth she had nurtured but with the vibrancy that transcended reality. It was her childhood once more, the days when the garden was a world of wonder, and she, a devoted explorer at her grandmother Cora's side.

In her dream, the garden glowed with a gentle luminescence. Each plant, each leaf under the moon's soft caress, spoke of love and care. Cora was there, her presence as comforting as it had always been, her hands tenderly tending to the earth. Young Emily watched. Her eyes were wide with the unbridled curiosity of youth.

"Grandmother, why does the garden seem so magical?" young Emily's voice echoed with innocence in the dream.

Cora paused, a small, knowing smile playing on her lips as she turned to Emily. "My dear, this garden is much like life itself. It senses the love and care given to it, thriving under the touch of those who cherish it."

"But how does it know, Grandmother?" she persisted, her child's mind grappling with the concept.

Cora chuckled softly, her eyes reflecting the moonlight. "The heart of the garden beats in harmony with ours. It's a special magic that grows from love, hope, and the earnest desire to nurture. You'll understand one day, Emily. You'll see."

The dream shifted, the images blurring around the edges, but the essence of her grandmother's words lingered, wrapping her like a warm embrace. She awoke with a start, the pre-dawn stillness of her bedroom greeting her, a stark contrast to the vivid dream. The remnants of sleep slowly receded, leaving behind a clarity that seemed both new and ancient.

Sitting up, she found Rosie lying beside her as if the doll had also been experiencing the dream. Emily held Rosie close, her heart heavy with the weight of her grandmother's words in her dream deep within her heart. It wasn't just a childhood fantasy. The garden's magic was real, tied to the love and care it received. She thought about the recent unexplainable phenomena, the rapid growth, the vibrant life bursting forth against all odds. It all made sense now. The garden was responding to her, to Maggie, Maya, Alex, and Liam's collective care and love.

As the first light of dawn filtered through the curtains, she sensed a profound connection to her grandmother, to the land, and to the very essence of life that played beneath the soil. Cora had known, had always known, that Emily would one day find her way back to this place of magic and healing. She would need the garden to help her heal.

Determined, she rose from her bed, her heart full of purpose. Today, she would walk among the plants and flowers with a new understanding, ready to embrace the garden's heart as her own, ready to nurture the magic that had been entrusted to her care.

Standing at the edge of the rejuvenated garden, the dream still vivid in her mind, the world around her was bathed in the morning sun's soft glow. Casting long shadows and illuminating the dew-kissed foliage. Her sanctuary of solace and rebirth seemed to pulsate with a life force that echoed her heartbeat, a symphony of nature that resonated with the very essence of her being.

Today, an unspoken vow swelled within her, a commitment to continue her grandmother Cora's legacy and deepen her connection with the earth beneath her feet. She realized the garden was not merely a patch of land to be cultivated but a living, breathing entity, a keeper of memories, and a source of unending wisdom.

She walked among the rows of burgeoning plants. Her hands brushed against the tender leaves, each touch a silent conversation between her soul and the earth. The vibrant colors of the flowers seemed more vivid than ever before, proof of the love and dedication that had been poured into the soul.

Emily paused by a lush rosebush, its blooms a dazzling shade of crimson. She remembered planting it with Maggie and Alex, the day filled with laughter and shared dreams. Now, as she gazed at the roses, she understood that their beauty was not by chance but by choice—the choice to believe, to hope, and to care.

She whispered to the garden, her voice a mere breath in the wind, "Thank you for showing me the way." It was a moment of profound gratitude, a recognition of the garden's role in her journey of healing and self-discovery.

In the morning's quiet, with the garden stretching out before her, there was a deep kinship with the land. It was as if her grandmother's spirit lingered in the air, guiding her hands and heart in the silent dance of growth and renewal. The garden had become a mirror, reflecting her own growth, her resilience in the face of life's trials.

Emily's thoughts drifted to Maya, the newcomer whose presence had brought an additional dimension to the circle. The garden had opened its arms to her, just as it had to Emily, Maggie, Liam, and Alex. It was a reminder that the garden's magic was not selective. It was universal, offering sanctuary and healing to all who sought it.

With renewed purpose, Emily knelt by the rosebush, her fingers gently tending to the surrounding soil. Each plant, each flower, was a chapter in the ongoing story of the garden, a story of second chances, of love reborn, and of the unbreakable bonds that tied her to this place.

Sounds of nature provided a harmonious backdrop to her work as the day unfolded. She planted new seeds with a gentle determination, each one a symbol of future growth, of potential yet to be realized. The garden, she knew, was a testament to the cycles of life, to the endless ebb and flow of beginnings and endings, of sorrows and joys.

Standing back, she surveyed the fruits of her labor, the vibrant tapestry of life that wove together the threads of past, present, and future. In this sacred space, she found not just the heartbeat of the garden but her own, beating in sync with the natural world around her, a rhythm of enduring love and endless possibilities. She remembered Maggie's words that the garden was in mourning for her grandmother. She was helping it heal just as it was helping her.

The sun climbed higher in the sky. A profound peace settled over Emily. The garden, with its myriad blooms and whispering leaves, was more than just a place of beauty. It was a gateway to the soul, a place where the heartbeat of the earth met the heart of man.

With Rosie in her place on the pillow and her grandmother Cora's wisdom guiding her, she stepped forward into the new day, into a journey of discovery and connection that transcended the boundaries of the seen and unseen. The garden awaited, its magic ever-present, a witness to the enduring power of love and the timeless bond between a granddaughter and her grandmother.

20

WHISPERS ON THE WIND

Warm golden light from the early afternoon sun highlighted the vibrant colors of the flowers and the lush greenery that had become Emily's sanctuary. A sense of peace enveloped her. A witness to the countless hours she had spent nurturing this space. Today, however, there was an air of anticipation, as if the garden was waiting for something extraordinary.

"You've been working hard today. The garden is truly flourishing." Maggie's voice drifted over, softened by distance.

Emily squinted, shading her eyes to discern Maggie's silhouette against the bright backdrop.

"I'll be right there! Save some seedlings for me," Maggie called out, sounding eager.

"The fairies left me plenty of seeds last night," Emily replied, feeling a lightness from the day's serene atmosphere. "Also, I'm brewing some tea. Hope you're in the mood for a break."

Stepping into the kitchen, Maya's arrival greeted her. "You're home early."

"It wasn't very busy at the market," Maya said, clearly disappointed. "I thought I would take a break and come help in the garden. I'll go back closer to dinner. It should pick up then."

"Perfect timing. Tea's almost ready. Maggie's joining us soon." Emily found comfort in the simplicity of these moments, the camaraderie that had blossomed alongside the garden.

Maya, offering to help, fetched glasses and filled them with ice while Emily poured the tea, the aromatic blend filling the air with a refreshing scent.

"Have you been in the garden all morning?" Maya inquired, her gaze falling on Emily's earth-stained hands.

"I have. It seemed to call me, more so after last night's dream. It's like visiting with my grandmother again, in a way," she shared, her voice tinged with nostalgia.

"Your grandmother would be proud of all the work you've put in. It's looking really nice. Everyone in town is talking about how you're restoring it." Maya handed her the glasses, and they stepped out onto the porch, where Maggie waited.

"Look who I found to help us for a little while," Emily announced, handing Maggie her tea.

"Hello, Maya." Maggie smiled. "How's the booth?"

"Quiet today. I'm hoping for better in the evening. Until then, I came to work in the garden." She glanced around. "It's incredible how this place comes to life. It's almost magical."

Maggie nodded, sipping her tea. "It truly is. There's something about this garden..."

Emily mulled over her dream. Spending time with her grandmother as they walked through the garden and how it thrived under those who touched and cherished it. "Being here, working the soil... it's like the garden shares its strength with me. It's more than peace. It's a profound sense of belonging," she confessed.

"I feel it too," Maggie said. "It's grounding, in a way,"

"Absolutely," Maya agreed. "It's my morning ritual now, spending a few moments here before facing the day. And I've been spreading the word about our efforts to save it from development."

Gratitude filled Emily's heart. "Thank you, Maya. That means a lot. We need all the help we can get." She pondered Alex's role in their fight against the developers. "Have you heard from Alex lately?"

Maggie shook her head.

"He stopped by my booth today," Maya offered, breaking into a slight smile. "He brought me donuts from my favorite vendor."

"That was nice of him," Emily said.

Maya nodded. "It was. The baby was craving them." She rubbed her hands over her growing belly.

"I believe you might have an admirer," Maggie said, setting her glass down.

"I can't think about that right now." Maya stood, attempting to change the conversation. "Let me add my touch to the garden. Maybe it'll bring some luck to the market later," she said, stepping into the lush foliage to join the chorus of life thriving under their care.

Emily pointed to a section where she sensed that working there would bring good fortune to her and those she cherished. "This area over there, Maya, it's special. Maybe working there will bring some luck to your booth later."

She disappeared to the section where Emily pointed, basket and trowel in hand.

"Wouldn't it be wonderful if Alex and Maya got together?" Emily smiled.

She and Maggie watched Maya disappear into the garden. Maggie turned to Emily with a knowing smile. "It's lovely to see new connections forming," she said. Then her tone turned slightly teasing, "Speaking of connections, have you thought about your own, Emily? With Liam, I mean. He's been a good friend to you through all this, hasn't he?"

There was a flush of warmth at the mention of his name. Emily looked away, focusing on the sunlit petals of a nearby rosebush, its blooms vibrant against the lush green. "Liam?" she murmured. "Yes, he has," she admitted. "But it's not what you're implying, Maggie. Liam...he's like this garden." She gestured vaguely toward the lush greenery. "Being with him, working with him—it's therapeutic. He understands nature, and somehow, it translates into understanding grief and healing."

Maggie nodded, sipping her tea thoughtfully. "He seems to light up when he's around you. And I've seen the way you look at him, too. Are you sure there's not a spark there, something beyond just friendship or partnership in this project?"

Emily considered her words, the soft buzz of bees around them lending a serene backdrop to their conversation. "Liam has helped me see that there's life after loss, that I can nurture new dreams, even if they're not the ones I originally had. With him, I sense a hope that is grounded in the present, not burdened by the past or anxious about the future."

Maggie reached out, placing a gentle hand on Emily's shoulder. "I'm glad you found him, Emily. It's important to have someone who can walk with you through the healing process without the weight of expectations. Just remember, it's okay to lean on someone like that, to find strength in friendship."

A sense of clarity dawned within her. "You're right, Maggie. I know some might expect or want this to turn into something it isn't. But I value what Liam and I have. Finding a friend who can help you heal just by being themselves is rare. Just like I found you, Maya, and Alex." Her eyes returned to the garden where Maya was diligently working. The garden was not just a symbol of renewal for the land but also for her own life. Perhaps it was indeed time to explore those quiet feelings, to give them a space to flourish. Emily was not just in a fight to save the garden but her personal life as well.

"I'm going to check with Alex and see what's going on with him and Maya. It'll give you some time to think." Maggie disappeared toward her house.

Left alone for a moment, Emily found herself drawn to where she'd planted the non-native seeds. A transformation had taken place. Overgrown with weeds, the secluded corner had erupted in a riot of colors, more vivid and breathtaking than any other part of the garden. Butterflies of every hue and birds with cheerful songs were attracted to this special enclave, creating a symphony of life that resonated with deep magic.

She marveled at the spectacle. The surrounding air glistened with an unseen energy. Tiny, luminescent orbs floated around her, whispering secrets in a language she couldn't quite understand but experienced deep in her soul. She reached out tentatively, and one orb landed gently on her palm, its light pulsating in rhythm with her heartbeat.

The garden had always been a place of beauty and healing, but now it seemed to possess a consciousness, a living essence that communicated with her through the whispers on the wind. She had an indescribable connection to the land, her grandmother, and the lineage of caretakers who had tended this earth before her.

In that moment of quiet communion, Emily realized that the garden was not merely responding to her care; it was a living entity, a guardian of memories and dreams bridging the gap between the seen and the unseen. The whispers on the wind guided her to create a place of unmatched beauty and opened her heart to the profound wisdom of nature and the spirits that dwelled within.

The garden, with its whispers and wonders, had become a sanctuary for all who entered, a source of joy, healing, and connection. Emily understood her journey was about more than cultivating plants and her grandmother's legacy. It was about nurturing the garden's soul, a sacred endeavor that linked her to the very essence of life itself. In the garden's embrace, under the watchful eyes around her, she found her place in the world, connected to the earth, the past, and the infinite possibilities of the future, all carried on the whispers of the wind.

"Maggie. Maya," she called out. "I know what our next step is to keep the developers at bay. We're opening the garden to the public so everyone can experience the beauty. If it can bring us peace, imagine what it can do for others."

The decision settled over her like a promise, binding her fate to the garden's future. She knew the road ahead would be fraught with challenges, but in that moment, inspired by the whispers, she stood ready to face whatever came her way. The garden, with its boundless beauty and hidden wisdom, had become more than just a sanctuary. It was a beacon of hope, a witness to the enduring power of nature and community, woven together by the unseen thread of love and determination.

21

AURA OF PEACE

A transformation had taken place. What was once a forgotten plot of land had become a sanctuary for all who entered its gates. The early efforts of Emily, along with Maggie, Liam, Alex, and Maya, had blossomed into a vibrant tapestry of life that now welcomed visitors from near and far. Even though it might not be completely restored, the decision to open the garden to the public had been met with an outpouring of support. A witness to the community's shared desire for a haven of peace and beauty.

Emily watched from a distance, observing visitors meandering through the paths lined with flowers and trees. Some walked slowly, with reverent steps, as if entering a sacred place. Others sat quietly among the blooms, their eyes closed, faces softened by the tranquility that enveloped them. The garden's aura of peace was noticeable, a gentle force that seemed to address the hearts of those it embraced.

"It's like the garden has a voice of its own," Maggie remarked, joining Emily on the bench overlooking the pond. "A voice that whispers needed words of comfort."

Emily nodded, her gaze lingering on a woman sitting beneath the old oak tree, her shoulders shaking with quiet sobs. "It's more than just the beauty of this place," she said aloud. "It's as if the garden recognizes the pain in people's hearts and offers solace."

Maya approached, overhearing their conversation. "I've noticed it too," she said, in awe. "A man stopped by my booth at the market yesterday. He told me he hadn't been at peace like this in years. Not since he lost his wife. He was brought to tears just sitting by the rose bushes."

Stories of comfort were becoming a common thread, weaving through the fabric of the garden's new life. Alex, who had been talking with other visitors near the entrance, joined them, his expression reflective. "There's a couple over there," he gestured toward the far end of the garden, "who told me they've been coming here every day since we opened. They said it's helping them mend their relationship, sitting quietly together, surrounded by all this..." He was unable to find the words to capture the essence of the garden's magic.

Liam entered the garden, his hand on the shoulder of a local child Emily knew only in passing. She watched the two exchange words before Liam joined them.

"Is he okay?" she asked.

Liam sighed. "He'll be fine. He's grappling with the loss of a beloved pet. He's heard stories of the garden and came hoping it would help."

The child moved silently among the blooms, his small shoulders hunched in a visage of grief that was noticeable even from a distance. Emily, Maggie, Maya, Liam, and Alex watched quietly, respecting the child's silent communion with nature.

The garden seemed to envelop the child in an embrace as he meandered the paths, stopping now and then to touch a flower or to watch a butterfly flit from petal to petal. The friends exchanged glances, each recognizing the sacredness of the moment unfolding before them.

Maya broke the silence, whispering, "There's something truly magical about this place. It's like it knows."

Emily nodded, her attention still on the child. She remembered the grief of her own losses, the pain that was once insurmountable until the garden worked its quiet magic on her heart. "It's more than magic," she replied. "it's empathy. This garden, it empathizes, it understands."

Having entered the garden shadowed by sorrow, the child now stood in the middle of the clearing, his face lifted to the sky, a smile breaking through the clouds of grief. It was a small, tentative smile, but it was the first genuine expression of joy he had shown since arriving.

The child's transformation was not lost on the friends. Maggie murmured, "Did you see that? The garden...it's comforted him, even if just a little."

Alex added, "It's not just the plants that grow and heal here. It's us, all of us. This place has a gift."

"We didn't just revive a garden," Emily said, her voice steady and filled with wonder. "We've nurtured a sanctuary, a place to soothe the heart and soul."

The child's steps were lighter when he left. His spirit visibly lifted. Emily knew that the garden's work was far-reaching. It wasn't confined to the blooming of flowers or the greening of leaves. It was a healer, a silent, steadfast presence that mended broken spirits and offered solace to those in need.

A surge of emotion overtook her as she absorbed their observations. The garden had become more than a project. It had become a living, breathing entity, imbued with the capacity to profoundly touch lives. "Grandmother Cora always said this land was special," she whispered, her voice barely audible over the gentle rustle of leaves. "I never fully understood what she meant until now."

The afternoon gave way to the golden hour, and the garden seemed to glow with an inner light. Visitors made their way to the exits, casting lingering glances back at the sanctuary that had offered them a moment of peace in a turbulent world.

The friends sat together in silence, each lost in thought, contemplating the invisible threads that connected them to this place and to each other. It had grown under their care but had nurtured them in return, healed them, and bound them together for a shared purpose.

Emily stood as the last visitor left. Her heart was full. "Let's continue to nurture this garden," she said, turning to her friends with a smile that mirrored the peace within her. "Not just for ourselves, but for everyone who finds their way here, seeking solace."

The sun dipped below the horizon, casting a soft light over the garden, and they understood the true nature of their endeavor. They were guardians of a sacred space, a place of refuge where the beauty of the earth spoke directly to the soul, offering comfort, healing, and an overwhelming sense of peace to all who entered.

The garden seemed to come alive with even more enchantment in the deepening twilight. Tiny, glowing orbs floated above the flowers, casting a soft, ethereal light. These were not mere fireflies but luminous garden sprites, guardians of its tranquility and magic. They flitted about, whispering to the plants and trees, their presence a soothing balm to the weary hearts that had visited throughout the day.

Emily and her friends watched in awe as the garden sprites performed their nightly dance. It was a mesmerizing display, the sprites weaving intricate patterns in the air, their light creating a tapestry of hope and serenity.

"Look at that," Maya whispered, her eyes wide with wonder as they stood there, bathed in the soft glow of the garden sprites. "It looks like the garden is celebrating with us."

Liam nodded, his gaze fixed on the glowing orbs. "It's a reminder of the magic that lies within this place, and within each of us."

A deep sense of gratitude surprised Emily. The garden had become a sanctuary not only for those who visited but also for those who cared for it. It was a place where the boundaries between the seen and the unseen blurred, where the magic of nature intertwined with the human spirit, creating a haven of peace and healing.

The whispers on the wind carried the garden's message far and wide, reaching the hearts of those in need. It was a message of hope, of renewal, and of the enduring power of love and community. United in their shared purpose, Emily and her friends knew they were part of something truly extraordinary. A living testament to the magic of the garden and the infinite possibilities it held.

The last rays of sunlight disappeared, and the garden sprites gathered around, forming a protective circle with their light. A warmth spread through Emily, a sense of belonging and connection that filled her heart with joy. She looked at her friends, their faces illuminated by the gentle glow, and knew they were all part of this magical journey together.

"Let's make a promise," she said softly, her voice filled with conviction. "To protect this garden, to nurture its magic, and to share its healing power with everyone who needs it."

Their hearts clearly aligned with hers. Her friends nodded and joined hands. Their bond was strengthened by the garden's magic and the shared commitment to its future.

While the garden sprites continued their dance around them, they sensed the true essence of its aura of peace. It was a place where dreams could take root, healing could begin, and nature's magic could transform lives. Together, they vowed to honor and protect this sacred space, knowing that the garden's whispers would guide them always.

22

THE WEIGHT OF SILENCE

The rough bark of the oak tree grounded Emily as she leaned into its steady presence. The memory of the previous day—the visitors, their laughter, their joy—swirled in her mind like petals on the wind. She had witnessed the garden's magic unfold, seen its power to heal, to offer comfort. People who arrived burdened by their pain left lighter, as if the garden had absorbed some of their sorrow. It had become a place of renewal for so many.

But not for her.

She ran her hand through the grass, feeling the cool earth beneath her fingertips. Not that she wasn't grateful for the garden or the solace it had brought to others. But as she thought about tomorrow, about returning to the house she once shared with Mark, a familiar ache bloomed in her chest. They had built that house on dreams of a family and a future that never came.

Her heart clenched as she thought of how, after everything, she couldn't give him what they both had longed for—a child. The garden could bring life from the soil, but her body had failed in the one way she most desperately wanted it to succeed. Tomorrow, she would see Mark and sign papers that would officially close a chapter of her life she hadn't fully let go of.

"Emily?" Liam's voice broke through her thoughts, gentle and unintrusive.

She looked up to see him approaching, his presence a quiet comfort in the morning's stillness. His kind eyes held a question, though he said nothing as he sat beside her, leaving enough space to let her decide whether to share her thoughts.

For a moment, neither spoke. The garden buzzed with the soft hum of life—bees weaving through the blooms, birds singing from hidden branches. It should have been soothing, but today, it felt like a reminder of everything she lacked.

"You've been quiet today," Liam finally said, his calm voice laced with concern.

Emily sighed, her gaze drifting to the blossoms swaying in the breeze. "Yesterday was beautiful, wasn't it? Watching everyone...the way they connected with the garden, how they seemed to find peace here."

He nodded. "It was. The garden has really become something special. You've created a space where people feel safe enough to heal, to let go of their burdens."

"But not mine." The words slipped out before she could stop them. She looked down at her hands, her voice growing quieter. "I've seen it happen to others, but for me...it's like the garden gives everyone else what they need, except me."

Liam frowned, not out of judgment, but the way he did when truly listening. "Why do you think that is?"

"Because what I need is something the garden can't give." Her breath hitched. "Mark and I...we wanted a family. I wanted to be a mother, to give him children. But I couldn't."

Liam's expression softened. "When we talked before, you said you feel you failed, Emily. That's not true."

"Didn't I?" She shook her head, emotion tightening her throat. "Tomorrow, I'll go back to our house. I'll sign those papers, and it'll all be over. And I keep thinking...if I could've just been able to give him that one thing, maybe we wouldn't have fallen apart."

Liam's hand hovered over hers before resting lightly, offering comfort but not pushing. "I don't think that's why things fell apart."

Swallowing hard, Emily blinked back the tears she'd been holding at bay. "Then why do I feel like this? Why can I watch other people heal and feel joy for them, but when I look at myself, I see nothing but loss?"

"Because you're still healing," Liam said softly. "You're still carrying so much. You can't compare your journey to theirs. They may have found some peace here, but that doesn't mean your own peace isn't on its way. You've been through more than most people understand. Grief doesn't have a timeline."

She looked at him, her vision blurring with unshed tears. "I thought this garden would fix me. That if I worked hard enough, if I poured enough of myself into it, I'd be able to grow something new. Something that would fill the emptiness."

Liam's thumb brushed her hand gently, a subtle grounding touch. "This garden is part of your healing, Emily. But it's not the whole. Healing isn't something you achieve by willing it into existence. It's messy. It takes time. And sometimes, it requires us to forgive ourselves."

The words settled over her, a balm she hadn't known she needed. She hadn't thought about forgiveness—not of Mark or the life they'd lost, but of herself. She had been holding on to the guilt of not being able to give him the family they'd dreamed of. The weight of not being enough.

"You deserve to heal too, Emily." His voice was quieter now, more intimate. "You've given so much to this garden, to others. But you need to give some of that love back to yourself."

An escaping tear trailed down her cheek. "I don't know if I know how."

"You don't have to do it alone," Liam whispered. "You have me, Maggie, the people who love this place. You've built something beautiful here, but it's okay to let others help you heal."

She squeezed his hand, grateful for his steady presence. The ache in her chest hadn't disappeared, but it felt a little less sharp. Maybe she hadn't found her peace yet, but maybe she was on her way.

As she sat under the oak tree, Emily closed her eyes and let the breeze wash over her. Tomorrow, she would face Mark. She would sign the papers. But today, in this garden that had witnessed so much growth, she would take the first steps toward healing her own heart.

23

THRESHOLDS REVISITED

Emily gripped the steering wheel with nervous anticipation as she navigated the streets that led to the home she and Mark shared. The home she had left to escape the suffocating feelings of failure that haunted her after their fertility struggles. The drive was surreal, each turn a reminder of a life that seemed both intimately familiar and painfully distant. The cityscape gave way to the residential calm of their neighborhood, where each house, each tree, seemed to hold a piece of their shared history.

She pulled up to the curb, and the sight of their house, with its welcoming façade and the garden they had tended together, struck a chord deep within her. The driveway, once a symbol of their journey, now served as a temporary threshold between her past and the uncertain future that lay ahead.

Bolstered by the resilience Liam had helped her cultivate, she took a deep breath. Emily sensed his presence, which was a comforting reminder that she would grow from pain. She opened the car door and stepped out into the crisp spring air filled with the promise of renewal. Each step toward the front door was a testament to her courage, a willingness to face the complexities of her emotions and the realities of a future she had never envisioned.

She unlocked the front door and stepped inside. "Mark." She called out his name, and it echoed through the entryway.

"You're here." Mark came down the steps and greeted her. "I'm sorry you had to come here. I wish this was something we could do through mail or email, but unfortunately, it has to be witnessed."

She hadn't been gone that long, but he seemed different somehow. She had forgotten how handsome he was. A few gray strands were showing in his dark brown hair. His deep-set hazel eyes appeared tired, hinting at sleepless nights. "I thought I could pick up a few things while I was here." Emily attempted a smile.

"Good. Then it won't be a wasted trip for you."

"I also get to see you again. That makes it worth it," she said, her heart racing.

"We have about an hour before we have to be at the lawyer's office. Would you like something to drink? Or you can gather what you want to take with you before we leave?" Mark asked.

"I would like to go through some things upstairs." She paused. "If you don't mind." Asking her husband for permission to go through her own house was strange.

"This is still your house, Emily. You're welcome to go through anything you want," Mark said.

"I don't know how this all works, Mark," she replied. "I've never been separated and on the verge of divorce before."

She waited, but he didn't comment. Emily climbed the stairs. Each step seemed to whisper memories of the life they'd built together. The once shared space now was like a museum of their past, each room a gallery of joyous and painful moments. She paused at their bedroom door, her heart heavy with the thought of crossing another threshold, one that was intensely personal and filled with echoes of their intimate relationship.

The room was as she had left it, a statement of the life they once shared. Emily moved through the space, touching mementos and personal items. The rug Mark bought for her after she complained of the wooden floors being cold, the caricature they had sketched on their honeymoon that hung above the dresser they scrimped pennies for when they first moved in together. Each a tangible connection to the life they had built. If she could, she would take them all with her. Instead, she gathered a few cherished belongings. The weight of the moment settled upon her. This was not just a physical sorting but an emotional reckoning. A sifting through the remnants of their past.

Descending the stairs with a small box of belongings, Emily found Mark in the kitchen, where they had spent countless evenings cooking and talking. The familiarity of the setting, coupled with the strangeness of their current circumstance, stirred a mixture of complex emotions within her.

"I made us some tea." Mark held a glass of iced tea for her to take. They sat at the kitchen table, a place that had once been the heart of their home. Where they'd shared dreams about building a family. As they talked, the conversation veered from the mundane details of the divorce to shared memories and laughter. It was a bittersweet acknowledgment of their history. A moment of connection amid the fragmentation of their relationship.

Seemingly more relaxed, Mark asked, "So, what have you been up to in Blue Ridge Haven? How is the farmhouse?"

Emily smiled, sensing a familiar warmth in his curiosity. "Actually, the garden has been keeping me busy. Grandmother's garden—it's a mess, but it's a beautiful mess. I've been restoring it, bringing it back to life with the help of some friends."

Mark looked surprised but intrigued. "Really? I remember how much you loved spending time there."

"I do love it." She agreed. "More than I thought. It's not just about gardening—it's about healing, about reconnecting with something deeper. With myself. The garden has a way of drawing people in, too. I've met some wonderful people who've helped me see things differently, helped me find a new perspective. Do you remember the Henderson property next to the farmhouse?" Emily asked.

"I think so," Mark said.

"I found out developers want to buy it. The people of Blue Ridge Haven are worried about what it will do to the community."

"What are their plans with the property?"

"I'm not sure. I've met the man who represents the developers, but their proposal hasn't been approved yet. I'm hoping it doesn't cause any problems with the garden or change the landscape."

Mark's eyes softened as he listened. "I hope so, too. It sounds like being there has been good for you. I always knew you had a knack for bringing things back to life. As much as I'd like you to stay here with me, I can see you need to be there a little longer." There was a pause before he added, almost wistfully, "I wish I could see it."

"You're welcome to visit anytime," she said softly, her heart skipping a beat. "I think you'd like it. It's a very calming place. You could meet everyone who's been helping me restore the garden. I met a young artist with a booth at the market. Her name is Maya. She was living out of her van. I invited her to stay with me until she can find another place to live. She's helping in the garden in exchange for room and board." Emily waited for Mark to tell her how she needed to be cautious.

Instead, he seemed to ponder her offer carefully, a thoughtful look crossing his face. "Maybe I will," he said finally, his voice filled with contemplation.

The reality of their appointment with the lawyer loomed over them. A reminder of the formalities awaiting them. In a spontaneous moment of mutual understanding, they said in unison, "Let's postpone the appointment."

"Are you sure that's what you want?" Emily asked.

"I'm positive." Mark took her hand in his. "I've never been surer of anything."

Neither one was ready to sever the last thread just yet. In the next few moments, it seemed like the past tension disappeared.

Mark stood and took her in his arms. "Stay here with me tonight. We could go to dinner at our favorite restaurant, and then...we can talk."

"I was hoping you would ask," Emily whispered as she nuzzled against his neck. "This is all I've ever wanted. To be here with you like this. Nothing else matters." It was as if none of the issues with her infertility mattered, and everything that went along with their struggle faded.

Their mutual desire for her to spend the night offered them a temporary reprieve, a chance to exist in the suspended reality of their past life together. For Emily, the night was a journey through the spectrum of her feelings—from nostalgia and sadness to acceptance and a glimmer of hope for the future.

The house seemed to hold its breath in the quiet night, a silent witness to the complexities of human emotions. They found solace in their shared vulnerability, a reminder of the deep bond that, despite the impending divorce, would always remain a part of them.

Lying in the guest room bed, a subtle shift in the air surprised her. As if the house itself were offering a gentle embrace. The garden's magic seemed to extend its reach, traveling with her to weave through the walls and into the very fabric of their home. She closed her eyes, allowing the sense of peace to wash over her, the garden's sprites whispering promises of hope and rekindling.

A sense of renewal came with the dawn, a gentle reminder that life, with all its complexities, continued. Emily woke to the soft light filtering through the curtains, sensing a strange mixture of peace and uncertainty. For a moment, she lay still, savoring the warmth of the bed, the familiar scent of their home.

Slipping out of bed quietly, she headed downstairs. As she reached the kitchen, she was surprised to find Mark already there, moving around with a quiet focus. He was at the stove, cooking with the simple grace that came from years of making breakfast together.

"Good morning," he greeted her with a warm smile as he noticed her. "I thought I'd make us breakfast before you go." He gestured to the stove where eggs were sizzling, a fresh pot of brewed coffee was on the counter, and two glasses of freshly squeezed orange juice sat on the table. "I thought we could use a bit of normalcy," he said, taking a seat across from her.

They ate in a comfortable silence, both savoring the moment. It was a minor act, but it spoke volumes—a quiet acknowledgment of their shared past and the tenderness that still lingered between them.

It was more than just breakfast. It was a reminder that, despite everything, there was still something worth holding on to, even if just for a little while longer.

As they finished eating, Mark reached across the table, his hand gently covering hers. "Emily," he began, his voice filled with a sincerity that touched her deeply, "whatever happens after today, I want you to know that I'm grateful for every moment we had together. And I'm proud of you—for finding your way, for being strong enough to face all of this. I know we have a lot of things to work through, but I think we're worth it. If you're willing to try, so am I."

Tears welled up in Emily's eyes as she squeezed his hand. "That means more to me than you know. I'm willing, and I think we're worth it too."

"I want you to take all the time you need. We can talk. Maybe I'll take you up on your invitation to visit the farmhouse, and you know, you're always welcome here." Mark winked.

They lingered after breakfast, savoring the moments together in the house that was their home. When it was finally time for her to leave, she stood by the door, gazing at the familiar rooms filled with memories. Mark walked her to her car, his hand resting lightly on her back in a gesture of comfort and support.

With a final wave, Emily pulled away from the house, watching it grow smaller in the rearview mirror. It was a symbol of her past but also a beacon of her newfound strength and resolve to embrace the future, whatever it may hold.

24

ROOTS AND RENEWAL

The journey back to the farmhouse was different this time as if Emily was seeing everything through a new lens, one tinted with the hues of hope and possibility. The rolling hills and lush landscapes of Blue Ridge Haven welcomed her, a stark contrast to the emotional terrain she had navigated in the city.

Wrapped in the golden light of the afternoon sun, the familiar silhouette of the farmhouse stood as a beacon of her newfound resolve as she pulled into the driveway. The vibrant garden, teeming with life, seemed to echo her inner transformation, a witness to the healing powers of nature and nurture. Tiny luminescent fairies flitted among the blooms, their delicate wings shimmering in the sunlight, adding a touch of enchantment to the scene.

Maggie was the first to greet her, her warm embrace a reminder of the support and friendship that had become a cornerstone of her life in Blue Ridge Haven. "We've missed you around here," Maggie said, her eyes reflecting genuine concern and curiosity. "How did everything go?"

Emily hesitated for a moment, the weight of her experiences in the city settling in her chest. "It was...more complicated than I expected," she began, her voice tinged with sadness. "Mark and I delayed the divorce."

Maggie's eyes widened in surprise, but she nodded, offering a supportive smile. "Sometimes, things need a little more time. How do you feel about it?"

"I'm not sure yet," Emily confessed, gazing out toward the garden. "But I needed to come back here, to this place, to really understand what I want moving forward."

Just then, Maya emerged from the garden, her hands stained with the earth and her face alight with the joy of creation. "Emily, you're back!" she exclaimed, wrapping her arms around her in a gentle hug. "The garden's been thriving, but it's missed its caretaker."

The three women walked toward the garden, where the fruits of their labor and love were evident in every bloom, every leaf that fluttered in the gentle breeze. Emily listened intently as Maggie and Maya shared updates on the garden's progress, the community events that had brought laughter and life to the space, and their plans for its future. Magical creatures, like tiny gnomes and sprites, peeked out from behind the flowers, their eyes twinkling with mischief and curiosity.

On a wooden bench amid the splendor, Emily shared her story. She detailed her journey to the city, the night spent in her former home with Mark, and the decision to pause the divorce proceedings. Maggie and Maya listened, their presence comforting to Emily's tumultuous emotions.

"It's strange," Emily mused, "how this garden, this place, has become such a pivotal part of my journey. It's like the roots I've put down here are helping me find my way even when I'm lost." She remembered something Liam had said during one of their long walks in the garden: every plant thrives on a bit of struggle. It's how they grow strong.

Maggie squeezed her hands, her gaze soft and understanding. "This place has a way of doing that. It's not just about growing plants, but about growing ourselves, finding strength in our roots and our connections to each other."

Maya nodded in agreement, her eyes sparkling with an unspoken wisdom. "And sometimes, growth means taking the time to understand our own hearts, to let them lead us where we need to go. It sounds like your heart was leading you when you were with Mark."

The sun dipped below the horizon and a profound sense of belonging filled her. Here, amid the growth and decay, nature's cycles mirrored her journey, reminding her that there was beauty, strength, and the possibility of renewal within uncertainty. The garden seemed to come alive in the twilight, the plants gently swaying as if whispering secrets to each other. The fairies' lights glowed brighter, creating a magical ambiance that enveloped them.

The words Maya said echoed in her mind, bringing a comforting clarity that maybe the best way to move forward was to embrace the uncertainties, much like the plants embracing the changing seasons.

The conversation lingered into the evening, the three women sharing stories, dreams, and the silent acknowledgment that they would be there for each other whatever the future held. Rooted in the love and resilience of their makeshift family and the garden that had brought them together. As they spoke, the garden sprites continued their gentle dance around them, a reminder of the magic and wonder that surrounded them.

Emily looked up at the stars beginning to twinkle in the sky, magic wrapping around her like a warm embrace. She knew that the journey ahead would not be easy, but with the support of friends and surrounded by enchantment, she was ready to face whatever came her way. With its mystical charm and timeless wisdom, the garden had become a sanctuary for her soul, a place where roots and renewal ran deep, connecting her to the earth and the endless possibilities of the future.

25

BRIDGING FUTURES

The community meeting was about to start, and Emily was filled with anticipation. Conceived as a forum to discuss the future of the Henderson property, it would be held under the sprawling branches of the ancient oak that had become a symbol of resilience and hope for her and her newfound family. The oak tree seemed to emanate a soft, comforting light, its leaves whispering secrets of the past and promises for the future.

Maggie and Maya were already bustling around, setting up the chairs in a semicircle facing a small makeshift podium they had cobbled together from old pallets and a sturdy plank. Liam appeared from a far corner and began helping. The air buzzed with conversation as neighbors and friends from around Blue Ridge Haven gathered, drawn by the promise of understanding what the future held for their beloved community. Tiny, glowing fairies fluttered around the oak tree, adding an air of enchantment to the evening.

Oliver made his way through the crowd, his demeanor calm but carrying an undercurrent of tension. As he approached, a knot tightened in Emily's stomach, unsure how the community would react to the plans he was about to unveil.

"Thank you for coming," Emily began, her voice steady as she addressed the gathering. The setting sun painted the scene in warm hues, lending an almost magical quality to the meeting. "Tonight, we're here to discuss something that affects us all—the development of the Henderson property. Oliver has kindly agreed to share the proposed plans and how they might affect our community."

Oliver stepped forward, clearing his throat before speaking. "Good evening, everyone. I want to start by saying that your concerns and the love you have for this place have not gone unnoticed. Our company is committed to finding a way forward that honors the character and needs of this community."

He placed an architectural drawing on an easel for everyone to see. The plans detailed a mixed-use development that, surprisingly, included green spaces, a community garden, and areas designated for local artisans and farmers.

"The idea," Oliver stood confidently, addressing the small group with a measured tone, "is not just to develop the land but to weave it into the existing fabric of Blue Ridge Haven, preserving its heritage while creating new opportunities for growth, collaboration, and connection."

Maya's eyes narrowed slightly as she leaned forward, putting Oliver on the spot. "We already have a thriving local market. How is this development going to be different? Will it take the place of the present market?"

His gaze met Maya's, holding it for a moment before speaking. "That's not our intention," Oliver assured her. "We're not here to take away what makes this community special. Our aim is to enhance what you already have. To make your local market bigger, where more vendors can showcase their goods and food vendors have space to expand without constraints." He paused, letting his words settle before continuing, "We're also proposing permanent structures for vendors—spaces they can rely on year-round instead of temporary setups that need to be dismantled. The goal is to provide a foundation that supports both the community and its traditions."

Not ready to let him off the hook just yet, Maya asked, "And what about the wildlife?" she pressed. "The animals that live on the Henderson property. What happens to them? Will they be protected, or are they just collateral damage?"

Oliver hesitated, then nodded thoughtfully. "That's an important concern, and it's something we're actively addressing in our plans. We're consulting with environmental experts to ensure that any development incorporates green spaces and preserves natural habitats. Wildlife corridors, native landscaping, and conservation areas are all part of the vision. The goal is to balance progress with preservation, so the land remains a sanctuary—not just for people, but for the creatures that call it home."

The crowd murmured, processing the information, their initial skepticism tempered by the unexpected consideration shown in the plans. The garden seemed to hum softly, a subtle sign of its approval or perhaps its magical influence over the meeting.

Maggie was the next to speak up. "This looks promising, but how can we ensure these plans will be carried out as presented? Our garden, our community—it's more than just land. It's our home."

The developer acknowledged her concerns with a nod. "I understand, and that's why we're here—to listen, to collaborate, and to make adjustments based on your feedback. This is just the beginning of a conversation, not the final word."

The community remained skeptical, and Emily noticed Liam moving forward, his expression serious. The ancient oak seemed to glow a little brighter as he approached the podium, casting a protective light over him.

"Liam," Oliver greeted with a nod.

"Oliver, the plans you've laid out tonight show promise, and the consideration for green spaces is appreciated," Liam began. "However, I'm deeply concerned about the ecological impact the development will have. How will construction adhere to sustainable practices? Specifically, are there provisions for preserving the native flora and integrating stormwater management systems that don't disrupt the local ecosystem?"

The question was met with murmurs from the crowd, as many

shared Liam's concerns about the environmental footprint of the new development. The garden seemed to respond as well. Flowers subtly turning their petals toward him and leaves accentuating his words with a gentle rustle.

Sensing a tension that went beyond the immediate concerns about the development, Emily watched the two men closely. She made a mental note to ask Liam about it later, curious about the underlying dynamics that might be at play.

Oliver adjusted his stance, prepared for such inquiries. "That's an excellent question, Liam, and I'm glad you brought it up. Our plan includes the use of environmentally friendly building materials and techniques. For stormwater, we're looking at bio-retention ponds and green roofs to manage runoff naturally. As for the flora, we intend to consult with local botanists to ensure that we're preserving and actively enhancing the native biodiversity."

Liam seemed unsatisfied. His jaw was tight. "Bio-retention ponds and green roofs are good starting points, but are you considering how increased construction will strain the local watershed? Your plans will disrupt habitats, and consulting botanists doesn't guarantee preservation."

Oliver's patience appeared to thin as he straightened his posture. "We understand the potential effects, which is why we're including expert consultation at every step. These decisions are not made lightly, and we intend to find a balance between preservation and progress."

"Progress shouldn't come at the expense of the community's values," Liam shot back, his tone no longer neutral. "Words are one thing, but actions speak louder. Will you commit to involving the community every step of the way?"

The crowd murmured their agreement, with several residents nodding in approval. Oliver hesitated, clearly aware of the pressure. "Yes," he conceded after a moment, "we'll include regular updates and feedback sessions with the community."

The palpable tension between them held the crowd's attention.

When Oliver stepped back from the podium, Liam returned to his seat with a slight nod to the community, having stirred their skepticism about the development's impact.

It became evident that Oliver's willingness to address these concerns directly had made a significant impact on the community's reception of the development plans as the meeting progressed. Emily noticed the atmosphere was cautiously optimistic, with many people more involved in the process, thanks to the openness spurred by Liam's pointed inquiry.

Emily, Maggie, and Maya shared relieved glances as the meeting came to a close. The night had not brought definitive answers, but it had sparked a dialogue, a crucial first step toward bridging the gap between preservation and progress.

The garden, bathed in the soft light of lanterns as the community members lingered to talk and share their thoughts, had once again proven to be a place of connection and hope. And for Emily, it underscored a valuable lesson—that even in the face of change, it was possible to find common ground and work toward a future that honored both the past and the promise of new beginnings.

The final rays of sunlight faded, and the garden's enchantment seemed to deepen. The fairies danced in the air, their tiny lights twinkling like stars. The ancient oak's branches swayed gently, whispering blessings over the gathered community. There was a surge of gratitude for the magic that had bound them all together, turning a simple piece of land into a sanctuary of dreams and possibilities.

With the meeting adjourned, Emily, Maggie, and Maya remained in the garden, their hearts lightened by the evening's events. They knew the journey ahead would be challenging, but with the garden's magic and their united spirit, they were ready to face whatever came their way.

Emily looked around at her friends and the garden that had become a beacon of hope. "Let's continue to nurture this place and our community," she said softly. "Together, we can create a future that honors our past and embraces the magic of new beginnings."

They stood together. The garden sprites joined them, their ethereal presence a testament to the unseen magic that wove through their lives. The ancient oak, the fairies, and the enchanted plants all seemed to sing in harmony, a silent promise that the garden's magic would always be there to guide and protect them.

No matter what challenges lay ahead, Emily knew they would overcome them. The garden's magic had bridged their futures, connecting them to the earth, to each other, and to the infinite possibilities that lay before them. And with that, they embraced the night, ready to face the dawn of a new day together.

The night air was cool as Emily approached the group where Liam and Oliver stood. The tension between them had been noticeable, and she couldn't help but think there was more to their dynamic than just differing opinions on development.

There was a tightness in Liam's jaw and a determined set to Oliver's shoulders. They exchanged a few more words, and Liam's eyes flashed with something Emily couldn't quite place. Their conversation was far from over.

"Thank you for your time tonight, Oliver," Emily interjected, stepping into the circle and hoping to diffuse some of the tension. "We appreciate your willingness to engage with the community."

Oliver nodded, his expression softening slightly as he turned to her. "Of course. I meant what I said. We want to work with you all to make this development beneficial for everyone."

Oliver walked away to speak with another group of residents. Emily turned to Liam. "Hey, can we talk for a minute?" she asked, trying to keep her tone light.

"Sure," Liam replied, though his expression remained serious.

They walked a short distance away from the crowd, finding a quiet spot near the ancient oak. Emily took a deep breath, choosing her words carefully. "I noticed the tension between you and Oliver tonight. Is everything okay?"

Liam sighed, running his hand through his hair. "It's complicated. There's more at stake here than just a development project."

Emily raised an eyebrow. "What do you mean?"

Liam hesitated, glancing around to make sure they were out of earshot. "There's a history between us, a long-standing feud that goes back generations. Oliver's family has always been involved in...let's say, less-than-honorable activities. They have a habit of prioritizing their own gain over the well-being of others."

Her eyes widened in shock. "That sounds serious. But what does it have to do with the garden?"

"It's very real," Liam said, his voice grave. "The land here is special, and there are those who want to exploit it for their own purposes. Oliver's ancestors tried to do that, and it caused a lot of harm. Now he's here, and I'm worried he might try the same thing."

A chill ran down Emily's spine. "Why didn't you tell me this before?"

"I didn't want to burden you with it. You already had enough worries of your own," he admitted. "But now, with Oliver actively involved in the development plans, I realized you need to know. The stakes are higher than just preserving the garden. We're fighting to protect something much more important."

Understanding dawned as Emily studied him. "Thank you for telling me. We need to work together to stop him."

Liam nodded, gratitude evident in his eyes. "You're right. And I appreciate you being open to hearing me out. I'll do my best to keep things professional and focused on what's best for the community."

"That's all I can ask," Emily replied, smiling. "We'll get through this, one way or another."

The ancient oak's branches swayed gently above them. A renewed sense of determination swept through her. Whatever challenges lay ahead, they would face them together with honesty and unity.

The night deepened and the garden slowly emptied of its visitors. A sense of peace settled over her. The tension between Liam and Oliver was something they would have to navigate carefully, but she was confident that with open communication and a shared commitment to the community, they could find a way forward.

With a last glance at the glowing lanterns and the ancient oak, Emily headed back to the farmhouse, ready to embrace whatever came next. The future was uncertain, but with friends like Liam, Maggie, Alex, and Maya by her side, she knew they would overcome any obstacle. Together, they would protect the garden and the spirit of Blue Ridge Haven, ensuring that its magic continued to thrive for generations to come.

26

UNFOLDING HORIZONS

The stage was set for revelations in the warmth of the farmhouse living room. Maya was visibly brimming with excitement and nervous anticipation. The soft flickering lantern light added a touch of enchantment to the cozy atmosphere.

"Is everything going well with your art?" Emily asked as she settled in the chair next to Maya.

"I was going to ask the same." Maggie sat beside Maya on the couch.

"Alex and I have been spending more time together," Maya began, her voice laced with a newfound softness, "I've realized how much we have in common. It's not just about sharing laughs or enjoying each other's company anymore. We've shared stories of our pasts, our hopes, and even our fears. It's as if I'm seeing him—and myself—in a completely new light."

Emily listened, her soul resonating with a mixture of joy and protective warmth. "I thought I noticed something different between you two."

"I know it sounds cliché, but it's like we've been drawing closer without even trying. There's this ease between us, a comfort I've never really felt with anyone else. It's terrifying and exhilarating all at once."

"What does Alex think about the baby?" Maggie asked. "It's not just you anymore."

"That's what I'm not sure about." Maya glanced at the floor, her voice a whisper. "Do you think I'm asking too much of him?"

Emily leaned forward, her voice filled with gentle support. "Maya, love and relationships, especially ones that grow in unexpected circumstances, are about navigating together. It's about understanding and accepting each other, not just the simple parts but the challenges too."

Her tone practical yet warm, Maggie added, "And it's important to communicate, Maya. Alex should know how you feel, and you should know his thoughts, too. It's about building a future together, considering both your feelings and the baby's."

Maya appeared to absorb their words, looking reassured and resolute. "You're right," she admitted, a determined glint in her eyes. "I've been so caught up in my fears. I haven't considered that Alex and I need to face this together. It's time we had an actual conversation about our future, including the baby."

The room filled with an air of solidarity. The three women shared a quiet moment of understanding. Maya showed a renewed sense of purpose. Magical fireflies danced in intricate patterns outside the window, adding an ethereal glow to the garden.

"You know the path ahead won't be without challenges, but with open hearts and minds, you and Alex can explore this unfolding horizon together, step by step," Emily assured her. "Have you started thinking about names yet?" she inquired, a soft smile playing on her lips, hoping to lighten the mood.

Maya's face lit up, a spark of excitement in her eyes. "Yes, actually. If it's a girl, I've been thinking about Lila, and for a boy, Ethan. There's something about those names that just seem right," she shared, her voice tinged with a maternal warmth that hadn't been there before.

Maggie shifted slightly, bringing a new angle into the conversation. "Have you thought about all the stuff you'll need? Like, a crib or a bassinet?"

"That's where I'm lost," Maya admitted, her excitement dimming. "I've been so caught up in the emotional side of things. I haven't really started on the practicalities."

Emily patted her arm with a reassuring touch. "That's what we're here for. Why don't we make a day of it? We can start looking for everything you need, from the crib to the cutest baby outfits."

The suggestion was met with an outpouring of gratitude from Maya. The discussion transitioned into a detailed planning session, each woman bringing her own strengths and perspectives to the table. They talked about baby showers, the merits of bassinets versus cribs, and the joy of selecting just the right items for Maya's new arrival. The magical fireflies outside the window seemed to listen in, their glow pulsating gently with the rhythm of their conversation.

Maya shared her excitement and plans as a subtle shadow passed over Emily. A fleeting moment of what could only be described as a twinge of jealousy. The discussions unearthed a silent yearning, a quiet acknowledgment of experiences she would never have. While her heart swelled with happiness for Maya, it also ached with a personal longing and emotional complexity. This twinge of jealousy wasn't bitter. It was a statement about her ability to feel deeply for her friend while confronting her own unfulfilled desires.

This chapter wasn't just about the logistics of preparing for a baby. It was a beautiful unfolding of sisterhood, support, and the shared joy of anticipation. There was not just talk of baby names and nursery essentials, but laughter, plans, and the love that binds people together through life's most significant moments. Outside, the fireflies' dance mirrored the magic of their friendship, a reminder that their bond was as enchanting and enduring as the garden they had nurtured together.

27

A DAWN OF A NEW BEGINNING

The sky was still a deep navy, speckled with the last of the night's stars, as Emily guided the car through the quiet roads. With its comforting presence and years of memories, the farmhouse faded into the background as they headed toward a new chapter. Beside her, Maya breathed through another contraction, gripping Emily's hand with a strength that spoke volumes of her inner turmoil and resilience.

"How are you holding up?" Emily asked, glancing from the road to Maya and back again. She tried to sound encouraging and not concerned.

Maya managed a shaky smile. "I'm okay," she panted, "just ready to meet this baby."

"We'll be there soon," Emily assured her, squeezing her hand gently. "Just hang on a little longer."

They arrived at the hospital, the early morning stillness of the place a stark contrast to the storm of emotions inside the car. Maggie was already there, her reliable presence calming. Alex, looking more nervous and excited than Emily had ever seen him, joined shortly, completing the circle that would surround Maya with love and support through this journey ahead.

In the labor room, time seemed to rush by while standing still. Emily watched as Maya, with a bravery that awed her, navigated each wave of pain. Maggie provided practical support, fetching water and ice cubes and speaking words of praise. Alex was a constant presence at Maya's side, his love noticeable with every touch, every word of encouragement. The room seemed to glow with a subtle, magical light, as if there was a comforting presence of the garden's sprites in the air, lending their strength to Maya.

A nurse entered, greeting Maya with a gentle smile, her demeanor professional yet warm. "How are we doing here?"

"Pretty nervous," Maya admitted, managing a weak smile despite the pain.

The nurse nodded understandingly, checking Maya's vitals with practiced ease. "You're doing great," she reassured her. "We'll take good care of you and your little one. Just let us know how we can make you more comfortable."

The nurse's calm competence appeared to relax Maya. She eased back against the pillows, taking Maggie's proffered hand and smiling up at Alex.

Meanwhile, Emily found herself in a role she hadn't expected. She became the anchor, the calm in the storm, offering soothing words, capturing precious moments with her camera, and ensuring the soon-to-be mother's wishes were respected. It was a dance of support, each taking turns to be there for Maya, to hold her hand, to whisper words to help her spirits. Above them, a delicate sparkle of enchanted dust floated, barely noticeable, adding a layer of protection and warmth.

Standing close to Maya, Alex took her hand in his, offering a squeeze of reassurance. "Everything's going to be alright," he said softly, locking eyes with her. "We're in this together, and soon, we'll be holding our little one. You're doing an amazing job." His words were a blend of encouragement and love, designed to provide comfort in a moment brimming with anticipation and anxiety.

Emily listened to Alex comfort Maya. Her heart was full. She imagined how Mark would be with her if she were in Maya's place.

Mark's desire to have a baby would have brought out every ounce of love he held within himself. She closed her eyes, letting herself imagine how it would be until her heart couldn't take anymore. A tear streamed down her cheek.

Maggie touched her arm. "Are you alright?" she asked, a hint of concern lacing her voice. "I know this must be hard on you, given your history."

Emily attempted a smile, trying to reassure Maggie she was fine even though she wasn't sure herself if she would make it through. "I'm...I'll be fine."

"If you need to step out for a few minutes, I'm sure Maya will understand. I'll tell her you needed some fresh air," Maggie offered.

"Thank you, but I'll be alright. I promise." Emily patted Maggie's hand. "Maya and her baby are the ones we need to be concerned with."

With Ethan's arrival, the room filled with a sense of completeness and purpose. Alex looked down at Ethan with a love that transcended biology. A testament to the chosen bonds that can be as strong, if not stronger, than those of blood.

They gathered around the new family. A profound sense of gratitude and love surrounded her. Yes, there was a twinge of something else too—a quiet longing, a what-if that lingered at the back of Emily's mind. But in that moment, the sheer joy of witnessing the birth of a new life, a life that they would all be part of in their own way, overshadowed it. The enchanted dust above them seemed to glow brighter as if celebrating this new life.

Emily and Maggie stepped back, allowing Maya and Alex to have their moment, yet deeply interconnected with the fabric of this new family. It was a beginning, not just for Maya but for all of them. A promise of new stories. New challenges. Endless possibilities. There was a renewal of hope in the hospital's quiet room, with the day turning to night again. A reaffirmation of the beauty and complexity of life itself.

Emily glanced back one last time as they left the hospital, noticing a gentle shimmer in the air, a reminder of the garden's magic that had followed them here. She knew that this new chapter would contain its own trials and triumphs, but with the support of her friends and the magic that bound them together, they would navigate it with grace and strength.

The dawn was breaking as they returned to the farmhouse, the first light of the new day casting a golden glow over the garden. A sense of peace washed over her, knowing that the garden's magic would continue to guide them, reminding them of the power of love, resilience, and the enduring bonds that tied them to each other and to the land they cherished.

28

HOMECOMING

Homecoming took on a new meaning as Emily watched Maya settle Ethan into the car seat, a task that proved to be a quiet battle against straps and buckles until Alex lent his hands, turning frustration into a small victory. In the backseat, Maya buckled her seatbelt and sighed with noticeable relief.

"I'm so glad to be out of the hospital," she confessed, the exhaustion in her voice hinting at nights interrupted by beeping machines and fluorescent lights rather than Ethan's cries. "I feel bad because I know Ethan will be up every few hours. I hate that he'll probably wake you."

Securing her own seatbelt, Emily turned to Maya with a smile that held both reassurance and a hint of anticipation. "We'll find a rhythm, you'll see. It's all good. Ethan is what's important. And you resting and recovering." After holding Ethan a few times in the hospital, she was in love. Despite the joy, each gentle cradle of Ethan stirred a soft pang in her heart, a reminder of her own unfulfilled dreams.

"You'll never know how much your generosity means to me...to us," Maya's voice cracked, bringing Emily back to the present.

"I love that I can do this for you. You've become family." Emily glanced at Maya in the rearview mirror, wiping away a tear.

"You and Maggie are the best thing that's happened to me in a long time," Maya said.

"What about Alex? He's pretty special, too." Emily chuckled.

"That goes without saying. He was such a rock during my labor and delivery. I couldn't have asked for anything more."

Maya and Emily both sighed as Ethan let out a brief cry.

"We'll be home soon," Emily whispered.

They settled into the warmth of the farmhouse living room. Ethan cuddled in a blanket on the couch while the two women gushed over him. The room seemed to glow with a magical warmth, the soft hum of the garden's magic seeping through the walls, bringing a sense of calm and peace.

"I don't want you to worry about the booth for a second, okay? I've got it covered," Emily said, her voice determined.

Maya looked up, a hint of concern in her eyes. "Are you sure? I mean, my art is peculiar. People have questions."

"I've watched you charm the socks off customers with your stories." Emily chuckled. "Just give me a rundown, and I'll handle the rest. Plus, it'll give me an excuse to brag about my incredibly talented friend. I'm sure Liam will be happy to help me. After all, he loves your art. He could go on and on about it."

Helping with the booth wasn't just a distraction. It was therapy. Emily found solace in staying connected with the community and being involved in something outside her own troubles. It grounded her, and each positive interaction was a step toward healing her own wounds, slowly closing the gaps left by her infertility and the initial faltering of her marriage to Mark.

"Maggie will be here to help you with Ethan. Between feeding and diaper changes, we'll be your biggest cheerleaders," Emily added, her tone bright but thoughtful.

Clearly overwhelmed by Emily's support, Maya managed a teary smile. "I don't know what I'd do without you two, and Liam, of course."

"Just focus on getting stronger and loving this little guy," Emily said, nodding toward Ethan. "We've got everything else under control."

"Alex said he would come over every day to check on me and Ethan. He even said when I got better, maybe we could come stay with him and give you a break."

"If you want to, that would be fine. I don't mind you staying here, but I know you and Alex are close and want to spend time together... the three of you." A twinge of regret enveloped her. She already missed Ethan.

"The three of us." Maya let Emily's words sink in. "That sounds so strange to hear. I always thought it would be me and baby...Ethan." She paused as she touched Ethan's hand. "Now there it will be me, Ethan, and Alex."

"You're happy about that, right?" Emily asked.

"Of course," Maya was quick to respond. "I'm thrilled about that."

"Alex is such a good man. He'll be a good example for Ethan."

"I'm hoping he will be more." Maya paused. "Maybe a father. I think Ethan and I would like that."

Emily wrapped her arms around her. "I'm so happy for you. I'll put some good thoughts out in the universe."

Their laughter and shared plans filled the room, a statement to the strength of their bond and their unwavering support for one another in this new chapter of their lives. Outside, the garden seemed to hum with approval, the flowers subtly turning their blooms toward the farmhouse as if listening in on the joy and solidarity within. Fireflies, aglow with a magical light, danced around the windows, adding an ethereal touch to the scene, promising that the garden's magic would always be there to protect and nurture them.

In the comforting glow of the farmhouse, surrounded by the love of their friends and the garden's magic, Emily, Maya, and Ethan embarked on this new journey together, their hearts filled with hope and the promise of endless possibilities.

29

WHISPERS BENEATH THE ART

The morning sun bathed Blue Ridge Haven in a warm glow as Emily made her way through the streets to Maya's art booth at the local market. The festival was in full swing, a statement about the town's collective spirit and creativity. With each step, there was more of a connection to this place, its people weaving their way into her heart. The air seemed charged with a hint of magic, an ancient energy that Emily had sensed ever since she began tending her grandmother's garden.

Emily stepped into Maya's booth with an overwhelming sense of duty and honor. Maya was in the tender postpartum phase, healing, and bonding with her newborn at the farmhouse. With Maggie and Alex checking in on her and Ethan, she knew it was a good use of her time to tend Maya's booth, relieving Maya of the worry about her only source of income while she healed.

Each piece of Maya's artwork showed her talent and vision. Emily couldn't help but sense a deeper connection to the world around her. The festival, buzzing with life, mirrored the new life Maya had brought into the world, adding layers to her reflections on growth, renewal, and the essence of community. The paintings seemed to tell secrets of the land, stories of ancient spirits, and forgotten tales that resonated deeply with Emily.

Then she saw Oliver. He was standing near the edge of the festival, partially concealed behind a booth draped with vibrant tapestries. His phone was pressed to his ear, his face a mask of calm professionalism. Something about his posture caught Emily's attention. It wasn't the relaxed demeanor she had seen before. There was a tension in the way he gripped his phone.

Curiosity got the better of her. With no customers at the booth, Emily stepped closer, pretending to admire a nearby pottery display.

Oliver's voice was low, measured, but carried a distinct note of urgency.

"No, listen, the micro-hotel isn't just another revenue stream—it's a statement project. The Henderson property is prime real estate. If we secure the permits quickly, we can begin clearing the land by next month."

Emily's breath caught. Clearing the land?

She leaned closer, straining to hear over the hum of the festival.

"I've already smoothed things over with the board," Oliver continued. "The environmental concerns are being addressed on paper—enough to satisfy the regulators. Once the trees are down, no one will care about what was there before. People only see what's built, not what's lost."

A wave of anger surged through Emily. She held her breath, her hands clenching into fists.

"Yes, I know the locals are attached to the land. That's why I've played nice. But sentiment doesn't pay bills, and it certainly doesn't drive tourism. The garden? It's a nice story, but stories don't bring in investors. This hotel will."

Emily's heart pounded as she processed his words. The garden, the community's charm, the people's deep connection to the land—it was all disposable to him, just another obstacle to bulldoze.

Oliver chuckled, the sound cold. "Oh, don't worry about the holdouts. They'll come around once they see the benefits. Or they won't.

Either way, it won't stop the project. Blue Ridge Haven is ripe for modernization, and I'm the one to bring it into the future."

Emily's resolve hardened. She could no longer remain an observer, hoping for the best. Her chest rose and fell with a steadying breath as she stepped out from behind the booth and into Oliver's line of sight.

She approached with a mixture of grace and firmness, the hum of Blue Ridge Haven's communal spirit pulsing behind her. "Oliver," she began, her voice carrying a note of caution, "I couldn't help but overhear your conversation. This community, our community, thrives on transparency and mutual respect. The plans for the Henderson property...have you considered their impact? On families, on local businesses, on the very soul of Blue Ridge Haven? Besides the fact you have been leading everyone to believe otherwise."

Just then, Liam approached, overhearing the tension in her voice. "What's going on here, Emily?"

"Tell him, Oliver. Tell Liam what your actual plans are." Emily stood in place, waiting for Oliver to speak.

"Yes, Oliver. Please do so." Liam waited for a response.

Oliver masked his surprise with a practiced smile. "Emily, Liam, I assure you, we're looking at the big picture. Development means progress and opportunities for everyone."

Undeterred, Emily pressed on. "But at what cost? Progress shouldn't come at the expense of our community's heart. Blue Ridge Haven is more than just a place. It's a living, breathing community. Newborns like Ethan deserve to grow up in a town that values its roots and each other. We're talking about the legacy we leave behind."

Liam nodded, standing firmly beside Emily. "And what about the environmental impact? You're talking about clearing land that's been carefully tended for decades. We need developments that reflect our values, not undermine them."

"Progress often requires change," Oliver said, his tone hardening. "This project will bring economic growth to Blue Ridge Haven. I'm not trying to undermine anything. I'm modernizing it."

"You have been lying to everyone in this community," Emily said. "You promised you would only improve what Blue Ridge Haven currently has. You didn't say you were going to change the landscape entirely." Emily paused for a moment, attempting to stay calm.

"I believe you owe everyone in this town an apology and an explanation," Liam added. "You can't just bulldoze over the existing culture in the name of economic growth."

Oliver adjusted his stance. "I can't change what has been planned for this development. Now, it's about securing permits to begin clearing the property."

"Clearing the Henderson property?" Emily repeated incredulously. "You're going to cut down all those trees and pull up the greenery. The Hendersons spent years planting and tending that property."

"That's what progress calls for, Emily. It calls for change. To go forward with our plans for the property, we need to clear it so we can build," Oliver explained.

Emily's emotions swirled into a stormy blend of dismay and determination. "You talk about progress, Oliver, but true progress doesn't erase the past. It builds upon it. It respects the land and its people. Like many in Blue Ridge Haven, the Hendersons have poured love and soul into this place. To simply clear it for something as fleeting as a micro-hotel...it's more than change. It's erasure."

Oliver's confident façade wavered under Emily's impassioned plea, and he attempted to justify his perspective. "Look, I understand the sentimental value of the land, but Blue Ridge Haven needs to grow. The hotel represents growth, jobs, tourism."

"But at what cost?" Liam echoed Emily's earlier question. "Once we strip away the town's charm and spirit, what's left? We have a chance to do something different here, Oliver. To work with the community, not against it."

Their heated yet hopeful exchange underscored a critical juncture for Blue Ridge Haven. Emily's and Liam's pleas for reconsideration of the project, appealing to Oliver's sense of legacy and community, left a palpable tension in the air. As they parted ways, the future of the Henderson property—and indeed, of Blue Ridge Haven itself—hung in the balance, a testament to the power of community advocacy in the face of development.

Tension lingered in the air as Emily and Liam returned to the booth. She glanced at Liam, his jaw still set, his eyes focused ahead.

"Liam," she began cautiously, "there's something more between you and Oliver, isn't there?"

He sighed, his shoulders relaxing slightly. "Yes, but it's a long story. Let's focus on the festival for now. We'll talk later."

Emily nodded, understanding that there were layers to this conflict she had yet to uncover. For now, she would channel her energy into protecting Blue Ridge Haven, knowing the battle was far from over.

The vibrant atmosphere of the festival seemed to push away the tension of the encounter with Oliver. But Emily's resolve remained firm. She would sort this out, and with Liam's help, ensure that the spirit of Blue Ridge Haven remained intact.

30

SEEDS OF UNITY

Under the shadow of impending change, the garden had become more than a sanctuary. It was now the battleground for Blue Ridge Haven's soul. Oliver's plans for the micro-hotel, with its stakes driven into the heart of the Henderson property, stood as a stark symbol of the community's fractured future. This was a call to arms for Emily and her allies—a challenge that awakened a fierce determination to protect their cherished way of life.

The initial shock of Oliver's betrayal had solidified into a steely resolve. With Maggie, Alex, Liam, and Maya by her side, Emily laid out a strategy that would extend beyond mere petitions and town hall meetings. They needed a campaign that could endure, adapt, and grow—much like the enchanted garden itself.

They convened under the ancient oak, whose leaves released secrets of the past. The garden's magic intertwined with their determination. "Our first step is clear," Emily declared during one of their strategy sessions. "We need to understand exactly what we're up against. That means digging into the specifics of Oliver's plans, the environmental impact assessments, and any potential legal loopholes. We'll work from a foundation of knowledge."

Maggie, her eyes reflecting the wisdom of age and perhaps a touch of magic, suggested, "We should also reach out to other towns that have faced similar developments. There's power in shared knowledge—and in shared resistance."

Always the practical one, Alex was already mapping out a more physical manifestation of their protest. "Let's organize a series of community-led workshops right here in the garden. We can cover sustainable living, the importance of green spaces, and the impact of urbanization. Make the garden the center of a living, breathing protest."

Maya saw an opportunity to capture the community's heart through art. "I'll curate a series of exhibitions, not just here, but in galleries and spaces around town. We'll showcase what's at stake if the hotel goes ahead—the loss of natural beauty and the disruption of our community fabric. Art can change minds." Her fingers traced intricate patterns in the air, and for a moment, the images seemed real, shimmering with a life of their own.

Having been quiet throughout the planning, Liam finally spoke up, his voice reflecting his deep connection to the land. "We need to remind people of the garden's role not just as a green space but as a community soul space. I can organize guided nature walks and talks about the ecological significance of the garden and similar spaces, drawing parallels that resonate deeply with our current challenge."

Buoyed by these plans, Emily recognized a personal step she needed to take—a call for help to someone whose expertise in environmental analysis could turn the tide in their favor. With a deep breath, she picked up her phone and dialed, the familiar digits igniting a flurry of emotions.

"Mark, it's Emily," she began, her voice giving away her nervousness. "I need your help."

The conversation that followed was a testament to the complexity of their relationship—strained yet underscored by an undeniable bond. Mark listened intently as Emily outlined the situation, the threat to the garden, and the broader implication for Blue Ridge Haven's community and environment.

"Blue Ridge Haven needs your help. The garden, our community, faces a threat we can't ignore."

"I'll be there," Mark said, his decision swift.

"Thank you. You don't know how much this means to me." Emily sighed. She didn't know if he was motivated by professional interest or unresolved feelings for her and the life they shared, but she accepted his help.

"I know how much your grandmother and her garden mean to you. I'll be happy to help if I can."

They disconnected, and a weight lifted from Emily's shoulders, replaced by a burgeoning hope. "Mark is coming to Blue Ridge Haven. His expertise on environmental impact could be the key to challenge Oliver's project effectively. Once we get that, we'll know exactly what we can do."

Word of Mark's involvement spread. The community's morale was buoyed. Their movement gained momentum, a tangible sense of unity and purpose emerging from the fear and uncertainty. They prepared for the road ahead, knowing well the challenges they faced but fortified by the strength of their collective resolve.

The days passed with a sense of urgency, the community coming together in ways large and small. Workshops filled the garden, art spoke from the walls of Blue Ridge Haven, and voices rose in unison against the encroaching development. And through it all, Emily stood at the heart, a conduit for the community's fears, hopes, and dreams for the future.

With Mark's arrival on the horizon, Blue Ridge Haven waited, caught between apprehension and hope. In its quiet splendor, the garden seemed to watch and wait too, a silent ally in the fight for its survival and the perseveration of a way of life cherished by all. At night, if one listened closely, the whispers of ancient spirits could be heard, guiding and guarding those who sought to protect the land.

31

UNLIKELY ALLIANCES

Under the soft glow of twilight, Emily stood amid the burgeoning life of her grandmother's garden, her thoughts a tapestry of concern and resolve. The sprawling green of the Henderson property kissed the edges of her garden and stood on the brink of transformation. The proposed development threatening to disrupt the delicate balance of the community's landscape. The challenge was formidable, requiring not just community spirit but the expertise that lay beyond her grasp. This realization led her to reach out to Mark, a bridge to a past they had carefully navigated in the wake of their separation.

Mark's arrival, therefore, was not a surprise but a planned collaboration, an echo of a partnership grounded in shared history and mutual respect. As he approached, the weight of their shared past and the potential of their united effort for the future lent gravity to the moment. The garden, sensing Mark's presence, seemed to come alive in a subtle yet profound way. Fireflies danced synchronously, and the flowers subtly shifted, their petals glowing with an otherworldly light.

"Emily," Mark greeted her, his voice blending professionalism and personal warmth. "I got here as soon as I could."

"Thank you for coming, Mark," Emily responded with genuine gratitude. The decision to call him had not been made lightly. When she left the city after her last visit, they delayed their divorce to give each of them time to work through their feelings.

That evening, as the last rays of sunlight danced through the leaves, casting patterns of light and shadow across their work, Emily and Mark sat side by side on the old wooden bench that overlooked the garden. It was a rare moment of stillness in their relentless campaign against the development. A soft, melodic hum filled the air as if the very essence of the garden was singing to them.

"I've been thinking," Emily began, breaking the comfortable silence that had settled between them, "about how much this garden means, not just to me, but to the entire community. It's more than a collection of plants and flowers. It's a living legacy of my grandmother's love for nature and her belief in the power of growth and renewal."

Mark nodded, turning to look at her, his expression thoughtful. "I can see that. This place...it has a soul shaped by generations of care and commitment. It's taught me a lot about what's truly important."

Their conversation drifted to the plans for the garden's future, to the dream of turning it into a community hub where people could learn about sustainable gardening practices, where children could play and discover the wonders of nature, and where older adults could find tranquility. As they spoke, the garden responded, the flowers blooming more brightly and the leaves rustling as if in agreement.

"It's a beautiful vision," Mark said, his voice filled with sincerity. "And I believe it's achievable, especially with the community rallying behind us. This fight against the development—it's not just about preserving land. It's about safeguarding a way of life, a connection to nature that's increasingly rare in our fast-paced world."

The first stars appeared in the sky as the evening turned into night. They returned to the farmhouse, their steps slow, reluctant to end the moment. Inside the warmth of the farmhouse, the day's end brought a new intimacy between Emily and Mark, a shared sense of purpose that gently rekindled the embers of their past affection. The house, filled with memories of Emily's grandmother and the echoes of Emily's childhood laughter, now welcomed Mark with an open embrace, silently acknowledging his role in this pivotal chapter of its history. A mutual, unspoken understanding hung in the air as they cleaned up the maps and documents scattered across the kitchen table.

Having traveled from the city intending to help Emily and the community, Mark hadn't arranged for a place to stay. The question of his accommodation had lingered, unaddressed amid the urgency of their cause.

Finally, Emily broke the silence, her voice soft yet laced with a newfound courage. "You know, you don't need to find a hotel. There's plenty of room here..." she trailed off, her suggestion hanging between them like a delicate thread. "Maya and Ethan are staying with Alex. The farmhouse is quiet."

Mark paused, his eyes meeting hers as if searching for any sign of hesitation. Finding none, he nodded, a gentle acceptance of her offer. "Are you sure? I don't want to impose," he said, his voice carrying a note of respect and a hint of the old familiarity that had once defined their relationship.

She smiled, a warm, genuine expression. "It's fine, really. I stayed in our home when I visited the city last time. It only makes sense for you to stay here with me. We're in this together, after all," she reassured him, her words bridging an uncertainty that had been hanging in the air since his arrival.

The decision for Mark to stay at the farmhouse, while practical on the surface, was a silent acknowledgment of their strengthening relationship. It was a testament to their comfort and trust in each other, a willingness to navigate the complexities of their past and present. Sharing their home in the city had been a surprise decision, but one not agreed to lightly. Here, in the quiet solitude of the farmhouse, it was a step toward something more profound, a tentative exploration of the connection they began rediscovering while in the city together.

The creak of the old wooden steps under their feet mirrored the tentative rhythm of Emily's thoughts. As they climbed, the familiar scents of aged wood and lavender wafted around her, carrying her back to those first nights she'd spent here after returning to the farmhouse. She had stayed in her old room then, unable to face the overwhelming presence of her grandmother's old bedroom, its memories too raw. But tonight was different. Tonight, she would sleep in the room that had once been her grandmother's sanctuary, drawing strength from its history.

Stopping outside her old bedroom, Emily paused, the weight of the moment settling over her. Turning to Mark, she gave a small, steady smile. "You can stay here," she said, opening the door. The room looked exactly as she'd left it—a space infused with her younger self's memories of carefree visits to the farmhouse.

Mark stepped inside, glancing around. His gaze lingered on the faded floral wallpaper and the stack of books she had abandoned years ago. "It feels like you," he said quietly, the warmth in his tone easing some of her nerves.

Emily nodded, her fingers brushing the doorframe as if grounding herself in the familiar wood. "It does," she admitted. "I stayed here when I first came back. But...tonight, I think I'm ready to sleep in Grandma's room. It feels like the right time."

Mark studied her for a moment, a flicker of understanding crossing his face. "That sounds fitting," he replied, his voice even as though he knew the significance of her choice.

"Goodnight, Mark," she said softly, stepping back.

"Goodnight, Emily," he replied, a thread of hope woven into his words. His kiss on her cheek lingered, gentle and warm, as if it carried an unspoken promise. Emily's heart fluttered with a mix of uncertainty and fragile hope.

As she walked to her grandmother's room, the memories of her first nights in the guest room mingled with a new sense of resolve. She'd come so far since those days of overwhelming loss, and now, with Mark in her old space and her in her grandmother's, it felt as though they were beginning to rewrite the farmhouse's story together.

The room welcomed her with a comforting silence, its moonlit corners embracing her in a quiet reassurance. Through the open window, the garden's faint hum reached her ears—a soothing lullaby of renewal and resilience. Emily slipped under the quilt that had once warmed her grandmother, letting the night carry her into dreams of second chances and shared growth.

In the ensuing days, Emily was surprised by how easily she and Mark slipped into a rhythm of collaboration. It was as though the distance and heartache melted away in the face of shared purpose. She had almost forgotten how natural it felt to have him beside her—his steady presence a grounding force amid the chaos. Watching him work with meticulous focus, pouring over data and analyzing their findings, Emily felt a flicker of something she hadn't dared to name in a long time: hope.

Her hands brushing against the soil as they tended the garden together during much-needed breaks, she wondered if this could be their second chance. Was this an opportunity to rediscover the reasons they had fallen in love in the first place? As he leaned over the papers spread across the kitchen table or offered a wry smile in response to one of her observations, she saw glimpses of the man who had once made her feel like anything was possible.

The farmhouse seemed to come alive with his presence as though it had been waiting for him to visit. The creak of the floorboards under his steps and the sound of his voice discussing environmental strategies blended seamlessly with the hum of the house, making it feel fuller, warmer. The garden seemed to respond in kind, the plants and flowers almost thriving under their shared care, as if nature sensed the fragile bond healing between them.

Mark's dedication to the environmental impact assessment and his careful collection and analysis of data gave Emily a glimmer of optimism. They had a real chance to protect the Henderson property and the garden. More than that, she wondered if the quiet moments they shared—the brush of their shoulders as they leaned over a map, the ease of their unspoken communication—were nurturing something, something worth fighting for just as fiercely as the surrounding land.

One late afternoon, as Emily and Mark pored over documents and maps, Liam approached them, a thoughtful expression on his face. "I believe there's something important you should see," he said, his voice carrying a sense of urgency.

Emily and Mark exchanged curious glances before following Liam through the garden. He led them to a secluded area near the heart of the garden, where the air seemed to hum with a gentle, magical energy. Liam knelt down, brushing aside some foliage to reveal a barely visible stream trickling through the undergrowth.

"This spring," Liam began, "is the lifeblood of this garden. It flows from the mountains and through the Henderson property, and nourishes everything here. Your grandmother knew its importance and protected it fiercely."

Emily's eyes widened as she listened, and a memory sparked in her mind. "We have to return to the farmhouse. There's something I need to show you."

As they arrived, she hurried back to the table where they had been working, her eyes scanning the collection of old journals she found in her grandmother's bedroom. She flipped through the pages, her fingers tracing the faded handwriting.

"Mark, Liam, look at this," Emily said, her voice tinged with excitement. She read aloud a passage that detailed the importance of the spring that fed the garden. Her grandmother had written about its origins. The journal entry was rich with descriptions of how vital the spring was, not just for the garden but for the entire ecosystem of the area.

Mark leaned in, his brow furrowing in concentration. "This is it, Emily. This is the key. If we can prove that the spring is essential to the garden and the surrounding environment, we might have a strong case against the development. It's not just about preserving the garden. It's about protecting a vital natural resource."

Emily's heart raced as they realized the significance of the discovery. The spring was more than a water source. It was the lifeblood of the garden, a connection to the natural world that her grandmother had cherished and nurtured. She glanced at Liam. His expression told her he knew more than he was saying. He led them to this discovery. A discovery that could save the garden.

"This is incredible," Liam said, his eyes bright with determination.

"We need to gather more data on the spring's flow and its impact on the local environment. If we can show that the development would disrupt the ecosystem, we might halt it through legal means," Mark explained. "I'll start compiling data on the spring's historical significance and role in the garden's health. We should also document testimonials from community members who can speak to its importance."

Liam agreed. "We'll need to present a united front. The community must understand that this fight isn't about preserving land—it's about safeguarding our heritage and natural resources."

In the days that followed, Emily, Mark, and Liam worked tirelessly to gather evidence and rally community support. They organized forums to disseminate the findings of Mark's environmental report, reinforcing the scientific basis for their opposition. Local media outlets, sensing the pulse of the community, questioned the viability of the development, lending a critical eye to Oliver's claims. They organized meetings, inviting residents to share their memories and knowledge of the spring and the garden. Each testimonial added weight to their cause, weaving a connection of personal and historical significance that underscored the need to protect the spring.

At one meeting, Maggie shared a poignant memory of how the spring had provided water during a drought many years ago, saving the garden and sustaining the community. Her story resonated deeply with those present, reinforcing the spring's importance.

"The spring that feeds our garden is not just a source of water—it is a symbol of our community's resilience and connection to the natural world. My grandmother understood its importance, and we must honor her legacy by protecting it. This development threatens the garden and the essence of Blue Ridge Haven. We have the power to make a difference, to stand up for what is right and ensure that future generations can experience the beauty and wonder of this place," Emily said.

Mark and Liam presented the data they had gathered, emphasizing the environmental impact and the legal grounds for halting the development. Their arguments were interesting, backed by scientific evidence and heartfelt testimonials.

32

THE CRUCIBLE OF CONSERVATION

A sense of anticipation hung thickly in the air as if the very walls of the town hall were leaning in to listen. Community members filled every available seat at the heart of this gathering, their expressions a mosaic of concern and hope. Standing behind a podium adorned with the emblem of Blue Ridge Haven, Mark prepared to present the culmination of weeks of rigorous environmental research.

Emily, seated in the front row beside Maggie, Liam, Alex and Maya, and other pivotal members of the garden preservation effort, watched Mark with apprehension. This moment was more than just a presentation. It was the embodiment of their shared efforts, a turning point in their campaign against Oliver's development plans for a micro-hotel that threatened the delicate balance of their beloved community and the sanctuary of the garden.

"As many of you know, the proposed development next to our cherished community garden poses a significant risk not only to the biodiversity of our area but also to the very fabric of what makes Blue Ridge Haven unique," Mark began, his steady voice commanding the room's attention. He used his laptop to cast images of the garden's lush landscapes on a screen, contrasted with stark, impersonal blueprints of the planned development.

With meticulous precision, Mark laid out his findings. He spoke of the spring that meandered through the Henderson property and into the garden, a vital artery of the local ecosystem that the construction and operation of a micro-hotel could irreversibly damage. His analysis detailed how such a development would disrupt the natural water flow from the spring, potentially leading to erosion, loss of habitat for native species, and a decrease in the natural filtration that maintained the clarity and purity of the water. As he spoke, the images on the screen seemed to glisten with an almost ethereal light, emphasizing the natural magic at stake.

Emily watched as he continued, highlighting the impact on local flora and fauna, drawing attention to several species that thrived in this untouched enclave, now at risk of displacement or extinction. Mark's report was not merely a collection of data. It was a narrative weaving together the story of a community at the crossroads of conservation and development.

Maggie leaned over to Emily. "He's doing a fantastic job, isn't he? Really drives the point home."

Emily nodded, her eyes briefly meeting Maggie's, a silent acknowledgment of Mark's impactful delivery. In the periphery of her vision, she noticed a faint, shimmering aura around the community members, a testament to their collective spirit and determination.

The room fell silent as Mark presented alternatives to the proposed development, suggesting modifications that could mitigate environmental impacts. His proposals were grounded in sustainable development practices, including green building designs, preserving natural waterways, and incorporating green spaces within the development itself.

Arms crossed, Alex whispered to the group, "We need to make sure everyone here understands the practical steps they can take to support these alternatives. It's not just about opposition, but about proposing viable, sustainable options."

Mark emphasized the importance of the community's role in decision-making. "This garden, and indeed the entire Henderson property, is more than just land. It's a statement to our values, to our commitment to preserving the beauty and integrity of Blue Ridge Haven for future generations," he stated, his gaze sweeping across the room, meeting the eyes of the town officials seated at the back. As he spoke, the emblem of Blue Ridge Haven behind him seemed to glow with a soft, otherworldly light, as if the town itself was lending its strength to their cause.

The floor opened for questions, and what followed was a fervent exchange between community members, town officials, and Mark. Emily watched, her heart swelling with mixed emotions. Fear for the garden's future, gratitude for Mark's unwavering support, and a burgeoning hope that their efforts might sway the tide in their favor.

Maya spoke up from her seat, her voice clear and resonant in the now quiet hall, "Your report paints a clear picture, Mark. How do we mobilize this information into community action?"

Mark nodded toward Maya, "Great question. It starts with gatherings like this one, spreading awareness and then organizing at the grassroots level. We must ensure our voices are heard not just in this hall but beyond."

Liam leaned over to Emily, whispering, "Did you ever imagine we'd get this far when we started?" His voice was low, filled with awe and a tinge of anxiety.

Emily shook her head, her eyes meeting his. "No, but I knew we had to try," she replied, her hands trembling slightly. "Thanks to you." A warmth spread through her, as if the spirit of her grandmother was guiding and encouraging her.

When the meeting adjourned, the community clustered around Mark and Emily, their voices a chorus of gratitude and renewed determination. They knew the path ahead would be fraught with challenges, but armed with Mark's comprehensive environmental impact report, they were empowered to advocate to preserve their community's character and natural heritage. The town hall seemed to echo with the whispers of ancient guardians blessing their efforts.

Emily reached for Mark's hand, a silent thank you for everything he had brought to their cause, for bridging the gap between past and present with such grace and dedication. Together, they faced the assembled crowd, united in their resolve to protect Blue Ridge Haven from the encroaching shadows of development. As they stood hand in hand, a gentle breeze stirred through the hall, carrying the scent of blooming flowers and the promise of renewal.

The battle for the Henderson property was far from over, but amid the shared fears and hopes of a community bound by a love for their land, a spark of hope was kindled. In the fight to preserve the essence of Blue Ridge Haven, they had found not just a cause but a common ground, a reminder of the enduring power of community and the unyielding spirit of nature itself. Now bathed in moonlight, the garden seemed to glow with a reassuring light, a beacon of their collective will and the magic that bound them together.

33

THE COUNTERMOVE

After Mark had laid bare the environmental consequences of the proposed micro-hotel development in the town hall meeting, Emily watched Oliver closely. His body language, once open and engaging, had shifted. His arms were crossed, an obvious barrier erected not just physically but symbolically between his intentions and the community's welfare. From her vantage point, she could almost see the wheels turning in his head, the cogs of counterstrategy clicking into place. Oliver's response wasn't immediate, but Emily knew it was coming. The few days between meetings would tell. The calm before the storm.

Emily's anticipation turned to reality. Seemingly unfazed by the community's pushback, Oliver launched into a series of calculated maneuvers. He commissioned a new environmental study, promising to address the concerns raised by Mark's report. Yet, Emily couldn't help but feel skeptical about its forthcoming results, wary of data that might be skewed to favor development over preservation.

"Have you seen this?" Emily murmured, scrolling through her phone, showing Oliver's latest post to Mark and Maggie. The image depicted a sleek, modern hotel surrounded by greenery, starkly contrasting the untouched beauty of the Henderson property. The photo seemed to glisten unnaturally, almost as if it were staged to make the proposed development appear more appealing.

"It's all smoke and mirrors," Mark replied, his tone laced with frustration. "We know the actual cost of their sustainable development."

Maggie leaned in; her expression was grim. "We need to counter this. The community deserves the truth."

Their resolve deepened when whispers of Oliver's upcoming meeting with local officials reached them. Gathering in Emily's living room, the air thick with concern, they planned their next steps. The garden, sensing their distress, seemed to hum softly, its magic providing a comforting presence.

"I can't believe he's trying to charm his way through this," Emily said, her voice tinged with disbelief as she encountered a post of Oliver shaking hands with a council member earlier that day.

"We've got something more powerful than charm," Mark promised. "We've got the truth and science on our side, and a community that's awake and united."

Liam, who had been quietly observing the dynamics, finally spoke, his tone reflective and solemn. "It's not just about stopping the hotel anymore. It's about affirming our values, about how we see and shape our future. Oliver thinks in terms of profits, but we're thinking in terms of generations. That's a narrative we need to amplify."

Liam's eyes glowed with a faint light as he spoke, a sign of his deep connection with the natural world.

A knock on the door interrupted their conversation. Emily opened it to find a neighbor, Joe, an avid gardener and frequent visitor to the community garden.

"I heard about the meetings Oliver's been having," Joe began, his usual jovial tone replaced by one of concern. "Is there anything we can do to help? The garden means a lot to all of us."

Emily smiled, touched by his offer. "Actually, yes. We're organizing a community forum tomorrow night. We need to share what we've learned and get everyone informed and involved."

"Count on me," Joe replied, his determination mirroring the collective spirit that had taken root in the community.

The night before the council decision, the community forum took place, and a buzzing hive of concerned citizens gathered to hear Emily, Mark, and Maggie present their findings. Now lit by hundreds of fireflies, the garden seemed to pulse with magical energy, reflecting the community's growing unity.

"As you can see," Emily addressed the crowd, pointing to a slide showing the garden's vibrant ecosystem, "the proposed development threatens more than just our garden. It threatens the very soul of Blue Ridge Haven."

A hand shot up in the audience. It belonged to a young mother who frequented the garden with her children. "What can we do to stop this? We can't let them take away our green spaces."

Mark took the question, his voice firm. "We need to show up tomorrow at the council meeting and make our voices heard. We must show that this isn't just about a piece of land. It's about our community, our environment, and our future."

The crowd erupted in agreement. A chorus of determined voices was ready to stand up for what they believed in. The air glowed with an almost palpable energy, as if the community's collective will was manifesting in a tangible form.

Emily sensed a swell of gratitude in the community's support as they left. Walking beside Mark, she leaned in, whispering, "Thank you for everything. We couldn't have done this without you."

Mark glanced at her, a soft smile playing on his lips. "We're in this together, Emily. No matter what happens tomorrow, we've already achieved something incredible."

They stayed to enjoy the cool night air, the stars above silent witnesses to their quiet resolve. Tomorrow's council meeting loomed large, but for tonight, they took solace in the unity and strength of their community, ready to face whatever the future held. As they walked through the garden, a gentle breeze rustled through the trees, carrying with it the faint sound of voices, as if the spirits of the land were blessing their endeavor.

Despite what she assumed was Oliver's formidable counteroffensive, Emily found strength in the community's unity. Once a personal sanctuary, the garden became a symbol of collective resistance. Together with Mark, Maggie, Liam, Maya, Alex, and a growing number of supporters, she prepared to meet Oliver's challenge head-on.

A deepening resolve filled Emily. Oliver's maneuvers, while clever, had inadvertently galvanized the community, turning passive observers into active defenders of their way of life. She found herself at the heart of a movement, her voice amplified by the chorus of those who shared her love for Blue Ridge Haven and its natural beauty.

The night before the council meeting, Emily lay awake, pondering the journey that had brought them to this point. The garden, with its vibrant blooms and whispering winds, seemed to offer silent encouragement. She thought of Oliver, not with animosity, but with a hopeful wish that he might yet see the value in preserving something truly irreplaceable.

Flanked by Mark and the community's most ardent supporters, Emily walked into the council chamber the next day carrying more than just documents and arguments. She bore the weight of a community's trust, the hopes of generations past and future, and the quiet determination that came from fighting for something bigger than oneself. As they entered, the sunlight streaming through the windows cast a golden glow, as if the very light was joining them in their fight.

34

A VICTORY FOR THE GARDEN'S HEART

Usually reserved for mundane municipal matters, the council chamber had transformed into a battleground for the soul of Blue Ridge Haven. Every seat was filled with latecomers lining the walls, a sea of determined faces united in a common cause. The air seemed to hum with a subtle, magical energy, as if the land's ancient spirits were present to witness the unfolding events.

Emily, Mark, Liam, and Maggie laid out their meticulously prepared documents and presentations, a tangible manifestation of hours of hard work and dedication. Settling into her seat, Emily scanned the room, recognizing many faces from the community forum. Their presence was a testament to the solidarity that had formed in opposition to the development project. She recognized a reassuring warmth, as if the garden's magic supported them.

The council members took their places at the front, and the mayor called the meeting to order with a rap of the gavel. After a brief introduction, Oliver was invited to present his case for the micro-hotel development. The tension in the room was palpable as Oliver took the floor, his smooth voice trying to weave a narrative of progress and sustainability. "Ladies and gentlemen, this development is not just a building. It's a future. A future where economic growth and environmental stewardship walk hand in hand."

Polite applause filled the room when he concluded, but there was skepticism on many faces. It was their turn now. Mark stood up and cleared his throat, his eyes scanning the room before landing on the council members. As he spoke, his laptop illuminated the screen behind him with images of the garden, the vibrant colors seeming almost to pulse with life.

"Thank you for your words, Oliver. But let's talk about the actual future at stake," Mark began, his tone respectful yet firm. "A future where our children can play in a garden that teaches them about nature, not just concrete landscapes."

He detailed the environmental impact with precision. Emily swelled with pride. The room was silent, hanging on his every word. When he finished, Emily stood, her heart pounding. She noticed a faint, glowing light around the edges of the room, almost like a protective aura.

"This garden," Emily said, her voice steady despite the tremors she was experiencing, "represents more than land. It represents our history, our community's spirit. Can we really stand by and watch that bulldozed for profit?"

A murmur of agreement rippled through the room. Standing slightly behind her, Liam added his voice, resonating with calm determination, "This isn't just about preserving green space. It's about maintaining the essence of what makes Blue Ridge Haven unique—its commitment to its roots and future."

Then, the floor opened for public comments. Mrs. Henderson, a longtime resident whose family had owned the contested property generations ago, stood up. "That land has been part of our community's soul for as long as I can remember. To see it preserved means more than you can imagine." A gentle breeze flowed through the hall as she spoke, carrying the scent of blooming flowers.

The mayor nodded solemnly. "Thank you, Mrs. Henderson. We'll take one last comment before we break."

A young boy, only ten, tugged at his mother's hand, urging her to stand. With a little encouragement, she did, lifting him so his voice could reach the microphone. "I like the garden more than my Xbox," he declared, and the room erupted into laughter and applause, the tension momentarily broken by his innocent candor. The child's words seemed to resonate with a truth that the adults had almost forgotten, reminding them of the simple, irreplaceable joys of nature.

A silent question hung over everyone's heads when the council reconvened after the recess. The mayor's voice broke the suspense, "Council members, please cast your votes."

Emily held her breath. Mark's hand found hers, their fingers intertwining instinctively. One by one, "No" filled the room, each one a beacon of hope. The energy in the room seemed to vibrate with a magical intensity, as if the very essence of the garden was present and rejoicing.

When the final vote was cast, the mayor announced, "The proposal for the micro-hotel development has been denied."

Cheers and claps thundered through the hall. Emily turned to Mark, her eyes glistening. "We really did it, didn't we?"

"We did, Emily. You led us here," Mark replied, his voice thick with emotion.

Maggie joined them, her smile wide. "This calls for a celebration! The garden remains ours!"

The community clustered around them as they exited the council chamber, their faces alight with victory and relief. Emily looked back at the council hall, then at the surrounding faces. "Today, we preserved more than just land. We preserved our community's heart. And this is just the beginning."

The victory at the council meeting was more than just a win against a development project. It was an affirmation of the community's values and a testament to the power of collective action. For Emily, it was also a deeply personal victory, a sign that hope and perseverance could prevail even in the face of seemingly insurmountable odds.

They returned to find the garden waiting quietly for them. This victory was just the beginning, a first step in the continued commitment to protect and cherish the natural beauty and heritage of Blue Ridge Haven for generations to come. The flowers in the garden seemed to bloom more brightly, the trees standing taller, as if celebrating the community's triumph. And as Emily walked through the garden, she could almost hear the whispers of ancient spirits, their voices filled with gratitude and blessing for the future.

Inside the farmhouse, the quietude was a balm to Emily's soul after the intensity of the day. She and Mark moved through the house, their footsteps soft on the wooden floors. The victory had not only saved the garden but reignited something between them. The time they had spent together gathering information and working to save the garden had drawn them closer, each moment a quiet mending of the unspoken fractures between them.

In the kitchen, Mark stopped Emily, his hand gently on her arm. "Emily," he said, his voice low and steady, "none of this would have been possible without your vision and determination. Watching you today...I remembered why I fell in love with you."

Her heart swelled, and she reached up to trace his cheek with her fingers. "We did this together, Mark. And I never stopped loving you."

Mark's brow furrowed slightly, his vulnerability breaking through. "I wasn't sure if we could ever find our way back. When I filed those papers...I thought I was doing the right thing for both of us. But every moment we've spent here, every step we've taken to save this garden, I've realized I don't want to be without you."

Emily's eyes brimmed with unshed tears. "I've thought about that day too—the papers. At first, I thought you were giving up, and it broke my heart. But being here, seeing you fight for something so important, for us—I know you've never stopped caring."

He cupped her face, his thumb brushing a stray tear from her cheek. "I've made mistakes. I let my grief build walls instead of leaning on you. But I want to try again. I want to fight for us like we fought for this garden."

Her voice trembled, soft yet resolute. "So do I. I don't know what our path will look like, but I know it's worth walking it together."

A quiet, shared understanding passed between them—a promise

to rebuild their relationship and the foundation of trust and love they once shared.

Without hesitation, Mark leaned down, his lips meeting hers in a tender and consuming kiss filled with the weight of their struggles and the hope of reconciliation.

Mark took her hand, his touch steady and sure, and led her up the stairs and down the hallway to his bedroom. The room, still filled with the echoes of Emily's past, felt like a sanctuary. Mark opened the door, the soft light from the hall spilling into the space as he turned to her, his gaze filled with a longing that mirrored her own.

Inside, they undressed slowly, savoring the intimacy of rediscovery. They spoke softly in the quiet moments between kisses, reaffirming their commitment to one another, promising to nurture what they had begun to heal.

Later, as the moonlight spilled across the farmhouse floor, Emily and Mark lay tangled in each other's arms. Their connection, renewed and deepened, felt as vibrant and alive as the garden they had fought to protect. For the first time in what seemed like years, Emily felt wholly at peace, cradled by love and the promise of a new beginning.

35

WHISPERS OF THE PAST

The victory at the council meeting left Emily with a profound sense of relief and accomplishment, a triumph shared with the community she had grown to love. Yet, the triumph was deeply personal too—a reminder of her connection to the land and the legacy of her grandmother, who had lovingly nurtured it. As she awoke the next morning wrapped in the quiet comfort of Mark's arms, Emily felt a rekindled warmth she had almost forgotten. Their reunion the night before had been more than physical—it was a reclaiming of their shared tenderness and strength, a sign that they too, were capable of renewal. This blend of victory and reconciliation inspired Emily to climb to the farmhouse attic that morning, searching for whispers of her grandmother's wisdom amid the scent of blooming flowers from the garden below.

She climbed the creaking wooden ladder. The attic door groaned open, revealing a space suffused with shafts of dusty sunlight that slanted through the small window. The room was a time capsule, cluttered with forgotten furniture draped in white sheets, boxes of old farm tools, and trunks that hinted at hidden treasures. The dust motes floating in the light seemed to dance with a hint of magic, casting a glow around the room.

Emily's gaze was drawn to a particular steamer trunk tucked in the corner under the eaves, its surface layered with years of dust and cobwebs that spoke of long neglect. Her hands trembled slightly with anticipation as she approached it, her heart pounding in her chest. She lifted the heavy lid with effort, the hinges protesting loudly.

More leather-bound journals were inside the trunk, wrapped in a faded floral shawl. They varied in size and wear, but unlike the ones she found in her grandmother's bedroom, they bore the meticulous care of someone who cherished their contents. Emily lifted them out gently, her fingers tracing the worn leather and the faded gold lettering on the spines.

Seated amid the relics of her grandmother's life, Emily read. The journals were filled with Cora's elegant handwriting, flowing across the pages with thoughtful observations, detailed drawings of garden plants, and recipes for herbal remedies. Cora's voice seemed to echo through the years, filling the musty attic air with her presence.

Twilight danced softly upon the petals and leaves. The garden's magic reveals itself in whispers and gentle caresses of the wind. Today, more than ever, a profound energy coursed through this sacred space—a sanctuary not just of flora but of souls seeking solace and healing.

The garden has always been a vessel for life's most potent magic. It's where the earth's quiet wisdom nurtures those who walk its path and tend to its needs. Here, among the ancient oaks and vibrant blossoms, the air is thick with the power to mend broken spirits and rejuvenate weary hearts.

As the first light kissed the dew-laden roses this morning, I planted a circle of forget-me-nots around the old willow. These delicate blooms, with their vivid blues and promises of remembrance, are my gift to those who find themselves lost in the shadows of grief. Let them stand as a beacon of hope, a reminder that love never truly leaves us, even in the darkest times.

The garden's magic lies in its ability to heal without words. It listens to the silent prayers of those in pain, offering its beauty as a balm to the soul. Each plant, each tree, carries within it a story of resilience and rebirth, teaching us that even after the harshest winter, spring will always return.

To any weary traveler who stumbles upon this place in search of peace, know that the garden awaits you with open arms. Its magic is not a thing of spells and potions but of love, patience, and the nurturing touch of those who believe in its virtues.

In times of sorrow, let the garden be your refuge. Sit beneath the willow, walk among the lavender, and let the tranquility of this place wrap you in its embrace. Here, you are never alone. The spirit of those who have loved this garden lingers, offering comfort and guidance.

May the magic of the garden soothe your pains, dry your tears, and fill your heart with light. Remember, healing is a journey, not a destination, and the garden is here to walk beside you every step of the way.

With all the love in my heart and the blessing of the earth,

Cora

One journal, however, was different. It was thicker and bound not just with leather but also with a palpable sense of purpose. Emily's breath caught as she turned the pages of a journal dedicated to the garden's celestial events. Each page revealed the mystical connection Cora had with the garden.

October 8, 1982

Tonight, the garden was alight with the ethereal glow of the supermoon, its silvery beams bathing each leaf, petal, and stone in an otherworldly light. The Lunar Blossom Festival was once again upon us, bringing forth the secrets hidden within the folds of nature. I'm deeply connected to the celestial cycles that govern this land and sense the magic woven into every inch of soil and every budding flower.

Anticipation filled the air as the moon reached its zenith. The familiar hum of energy enveloped the garden like a whispering breeze, revealing patterns and pathways normally invisible to the casual observer. Beneath the glowing blossoms, the guardian spirit appeared—a figure of light and serenity whose radiance seemed to seep into the very earth itself. This celestial being, whose presence graces us only on this sacred night, moved gracefully among the flowers, leaving trails of luminous energy that touched the soul of every living thing. Each plant seemed to straighten with renewed vigor, each flower unfurling its petals wider as if in reverence.

I watched in awe as the guardian spirit brought healing to the wilting blooms and coaxed new life from the soil, its touch both gentle and invigorating. It was a reminder of the immense power hidden within nature and the harmonious connection we must nurture with it. The spirit's blessing permeated every corner of the garden, offering peace and renewal to the plants and all who tended them with love and care.

According to the cycles of the moon, this celestial alignment returns every twenty-one years. The next Lunar Blossom Festival will occur on September 15, 2003, October 22, 2024, and every twenty-one years after. I trust that this knowledge will be preserved for future generations and that my beloved Emily will one day be ready to embrace its magic and power.

As I write these words, I can still feel the warmth of the spirit's glow, and I know that the garden will thrive in the coming days. This sacred event is a reminder of the cyclical dance of the moon and the earth, a promise of rebirth and transformation. I hope the next Lunar Blossom Festival will be a beacon of hope for all seeking solace within these sacred grounds.

With love and gratitude,

Cora

Emily's eyes widened with wonder and a deep, resonant connection. She realized the garden held more mysteries and powers than she had ever imagined. Cora's entries spoke of specific dates and alignments. The next occurrence of this celestial event was not far off.

Inspired by her grandmother's writings, an overwhelming urge to share this part of Cora's legacy with her close friends overcame her. She would invite Maggie, Maya, Alex, Liam, and Mark to join her in witnessing the upcoming Lunar Blossom Festival.

Emily closed the journal, her mind alive with possibilities. There was a profound connection not only to her grandmother but also to the garden itself. It was as if she had uncovered the missing piece of a puzzle that her grandmother had left for her to find.

With the journals tucked under her arm, Emily descended the ladder, her steps light with anticipation. The discovery of her grandmother's journals was not just a link to her past but a gateway to a magical experience that promised to bring healing and wonder to all who were open to the garden's mysteries.

36

THE INVITATION

After discovering her grandmother's journals, Emily experienced a surge of excitement and a deep sense of purpose. The garden was not just a place of beauty and tranquility. It was a living legacy, filled with celestial mysteries that were waiting to be revealed. With the upcoming Lunar Blossom Festival drawing near, Emily knew this was the perfect time to share her discovery with her closest friends.

Later that afternoon, she arranged a small gathering at the farmhouse. She and Mark prepared a simple tea service on the rustic wooden table, setting out Cora's journals next to an arrangement of wildflowers picked from the garden. The flowers seemed to emit a faint, magical glow, their colors more vibrant than usual, as if they sensed the significance of the upcoming event.

One by one, Maggie, Maya, and Alex arrived, bringing a sense of warmth and camaraderie into the cozy kitchen. Emily and Mark greeted them with hugs. Emily's eyes were bright with anticipation. As small talk ensued and everyone settled around the table, Emily caught sight of Mark, now seated on the living room floor, with Maya's baby, Ethan, gurgling happily in his lap.

Emily's smile faltered as she watched them, the scene sharpening the ache of her own longing to give Mark a child, to see him be the father she knew he could be. The love and potential she saw in these moments made her reconsider their decision to reconcile, stirring doubts about the path they had chosen.

Turning back to her friends, Emily cleared her throat, drawing attention to the journals. "Thank you all for coming," she began, her voice tinged with excitement as everyone settled around the table. "I've found something incredible in the attic. More of Grandmother Cora's journals."

The conversation turned to the celestial phenomena described in Cora's writings. Emily took part but remained fixated on Mark and Ethan, the tender image a poignant reminder of what could never be.

"What I discovered is this one is no ordinary journal." She picked up the thicker journal. "It describes a celestial event that happens right here in our garden."

Her friends exchanged intrigued glances, leaning in closer as Emily opened the worn leather cover of the journal. She turned the pages to a detailed entry about the Lunar Blossom Festival, her finger tracing the lines of Cora's elegant handwriting.

"Grandmother wrote about a night when the garden transforms under a supermoon that glows with a mystical light," Emily continued, her voice filled with wonder. "Flowers bloom that aren't seen at any other time, and there's a guardian spirit that appears to bring healing and renewal."

Maggie's eyes widened, showing the story captivated her. "That sounds like something out of a fairy tale," she said, her skepticism softened by the earnestness of Emily's tone.

"It does," Emily agreed, smiling gently. "But I believe it's real. The way Grandmother describes it, I can almost see it. And there's more. According to Grandmother, the next occurrence is just a week away. I want us all to experience it together."

Maya, who had been quietly listening, spoke up, her voice thoughtful, "It's like we've always said. The garden has its own heartbeat, and we're being invited to feel its pulse."

Alex, ever the pragmatist, nodded slowly. "It's an incredible opportunity to see if there's scientific evidence behind this phenomenon. I'm in."

Her friends expressed their intrigue and excitement. A mix of joy and sorrow overcame her. The festival would be a magical night, yet her heart was heavy with unspoken fears and unfulfilled dreams.

Mark finally joined the group, handing Ethan back to Maya with a reluctant smile. He reached for Emily's hand, giving it a reassuring squeeze. "I have to return to the city for work, but I promise to be back in time for this. It sounds like a once-in-a-lifetime experience. I wouldn't miss it for the world."

"Actually, I also invited Liam, but he sent his regrets earlier today," Emily interjected, a hint of disappointment in her voice. "He was called away on an urgent matter and won't be able to join us. He seemed really apologetic about it. I'll tell him what we talked about tonight."

"I'm sorry he couldn't make it. I hope everything is all right," Maggie said.

"I asked him the same thing. He said it was a customer he needed to help with a project. He would be back soon," Emily explained.

Heartened by their responses, Emily proposed they meet again on the evening of the event. "I'll set up lanterns and blankets in the garden so we can all watch the stars and wait for the garden to reveal its secrets," she suggested, her mind already envisioning the magical night.

The meeting concluded and her friends left. There was a profound sense of connection. Not just to the people she cared about but to the garden and her grandmother's legacy. She cleared away the dishes as Mark skimmed through the journal, reading passages he found interesting. Her thoughts lingered on the family she longed to create with Mark, wondering if the celestial event might somehow renew not just the garden but their hopes and dreams as well.

"This sounds amazing," he said. "I can't believe your grandmother never mentioned this to you before. You guys were so close. She told you everything."

Emily shrugged. "Maybe she didn't think I would believe her.

Besides, it only happens at certain times. I probably wasn't around during the events."

"That's true." Mark nodded as he moved toward Emily, slipping his arms around her waist. "I promise to be here for it, but right now, I think we should go to bed. Since I leave tomorrow..." he kissed her neck.

Emily leaned into him and sighed. "I like that idea."

After Mark left for the city, she spent the next few days preparing. Hanging lanterns that cast soft glows among the foliage and gathering cozy blankets and cushions to spread around the garden the night of the event. The lanterns, imbued with a touch of the garden's magic, glowed with a gentle luminescence that seemed to breathe with the rhythm of the garden.

Tending to each detail with care, ensuring that the night would be perfect. The garden was quiet, the flowers nodding gently in the breeze, as if in anticipation of the event.

Each day before the festival, Emily walked through the garden, checking each lantern, deciding each placement of the blankets, ensuring everything was ready. As the sun set, casting long shadows and painting the garden in hues of orange and gold, Emily stood back to admire her work. She could almost sense the garden's approval, the plants and flowers seeming to shimmer with anticipation.

The stage was set for a night of wonder, a gathering that would bridge the past with the present and, perhaps, open the door to new beginnings. The garden waited in quiet hope, and so did Emily, her heart full of hope and her spirit attuned to the unfolding mysteries of the celestial night that awaited them. The promise of magic was in the air, the very essence of the garden poised to reveal its deepest secrets under the light of the supermoon.

37

SHADOWS IN THE SUNRISE

The first rays of dawn streaked across the sky as Emily knelt in the garden, her hands deep in the rich, moist soil, planting the seeds left in the basket overnight. Around her, early morning light played upon the leaves and petals, bathing everything in a gentle amber glow. The flowers seemed to nod in approval, their petals glowing with a faint, magical light that hinted at the garden's secrets.

Her focus was intent on the earth before her, on nurturing the tender shoots that sprouted with promise. Yet, her brow was furrowed, her movements slightly more forceful than necessary. There was a weight on her heart, a shadow that lingered even as the surrounding garden flourished. She was lost in thoughts that had kept her awake all night and still disturbed her. The image of Mark tending to Ethan. The joy on his face as Ethan smiled and cooed was something she could only dream about.

Arriving to lend a hand with the new saplings, Liam approached quietly. "Morning, Emily," he called out softly.

She looked up, managing a small smile. "Liam, good morning. I didn't see you there."

He stepped closer, setting down his gardening tools. "You seem a bit preoccupied this morning. Anything you want to talk about?" His voice was gentle, inviting confidence without pushing too hard.

She hesitated, a part of her wanting to keep her worries locked away. Yet, the concern in Liam's eyes and the garden's peacefulness made her want to open up. "It's about Mark and me," she finally admitted, her voice barely above a whisper.

Liam knelt beside her, his presence reassuring. "What's going on?"

Emily paused her work, her hands resting on the soil. "We've reconciled," she began, a mix of joy and vulnerability in her tone. "Mark and I have called off the divorce."

Liam nodded, his gaze steady and encouraging. "That's a powerful thing. Rebuilding that connection must have taken courage for both of you."

She smiled faintly, her fingers tracing the edge of a nearby leaf. "It did. But as much as we've come together, there's still a shadow hanging over us. The issue of children hasn't gone away. Watching him with Ethan the other day, it broke my heart in a way I didn't expect. I saw how much joy it brought him, and I couldn't help wondering if I'll always be the reason he doesn't get to be a father."

Liam placed a hand on her shoulder, his touch grounding. "Emily, it's clear that Mark loves you deeply. You've both chosen to fight for each other despite the pain you've been through. That says more than any single obstacle could. Have you talked to him about how you're feeling?"

She nodded slowly. "We've talked about adoption before, after IVF didn't work. But...I'm scared. What if it's too much for us? What if it pushes us apart again?"

"Life is full of uncertainties," Liam said thoughtfully. "But it sounds like you're already taking the first steps—choosing to face those uncertainties together. That means something if you've found your way back to each other after everything. It means you have a foundation worth fighting for."

Emily's heart lightened, the weight of her fears easing slightly. "You're right. Rebuilding what we have has been worth every painful step. Maybe it's time to have that conversation with him again, to be open about what's next for us."

Liam smiled, squeezing her shoulder reassuringly. "Whatever happens, remember you're not alone in this. You've got Mark, and you've got a whole community rooting for you. And this garden. It's a testament to what love and perseverance can create, even in the face of challenges."

As the sun rose higher, bathing the garden in warm light, Emily felt a renewed resolve. The surrounding greenery seemed to echo her determination, the flowers nodding gently as if in agreement. "Thank you, Liam," she said. "I think I needed to hear that. It's time to move forward—not just for Mark and me, but for everything we've built together."

He helped her to her feet. There was a renewed sense of resolve inside her. The surrounding garden was a testament to growth and resilience, reminding her that, like the plants she tended so lovingly, she too could thrive despite the challenges.

"Let me show you the area I've set up for the festival." Emily led him down the path toward the beautifully decorated area. The glow of the garden grew brighter as they walked, the flowers whispering softly in the morning breeze, their magic a comforting presence.

However, as they approached the festively adorned section of the garden, Liam paused at the edge, a subtle tension visible in his posture. He scanned the arrangement with a careful, almost calculated gaze, his expression unreadable.

Emily noticed his hesitation. "Is something wrong?" she asked, her voice laced with concern. Her excitement about showing her preparations waned slightly, replaced by curiosity at his reaction.

Liam turned to her, a gentle smile masking the complexity of his thoughts. "It's nothing, Emily. Everything looks wonderful," he assured her, but his voice carried a careful note, as if he were weighing every word. "You've done an incredible job with the setup."

Emily studied his face, looking for a clue to his restraint. "You seem...distant. Are you sure everything is okay?"

Liam glanced back at the setup, then met her eyes with a sincerity that momentarily veiled his inner conflict. "I'm just a bit preoccupied with some personal matters," he said, his tone attempting casualness. "But I'm really looking forward to the event. It's going to be a special night."

"I thought maybe Oliver's scarcity lately might have lightened your mood." She nodded, accepting his explanation, though part of her remained unconvinced. There was something he wasn't telling her, a secret that seemed almost palpable in his careful avoidance of the area she had so lovingly prepared. "Well, if there's anything you want to talk about, I'm here just like you said you were here for me," she offered, hoping to provide him with the same support he had given her.

Liam accepted her offer with a warm, appreciative nod. "Thank you. That means a lot."

They walked back toward the main part of the garden, the early morning peace enveloping them once again. As they parted ways, Emily's mind buzzed with unanswered questions. Liam's unusual behavior added an unexpected layer of mystery to the upcoming event. Whatever reservations he harbored, Emily sensed they were connected to the Lunar Blossom Festival, so she couldn't yet understand.

The day drew to a close, and Emily found herself increasingly intrigued by Liam's actions and words. There was a depth to him she had not seen before, a complexity that seemed intrinsically linked to the garden's hidden legacies. With every preparation, every lantern hung, and every blanket laid, her anticipation grew not just for the celestial phenomena but also for the revelations that the night might bring about Liam, the garden, and the mystical legacy her grandmother had left behind.

The garden waited in silence, and so did Emily, her heart full of hope and her spirit attuned to the unfolding mysteries of the celestial night that awaited them. The flowers glowed faintly in the twilight, as if sharing her excitement, and the whispers of the past seemed to grow louder, promising secrets and magic yet to be revealed.

38

PAST ECHOES

The sun had dipped below the horizon, and a golden glow filtered through the farmhouse's windows. The world outside was quiet, but inside, Emily's mind buzzed with restless curiosity. Seated at the old oak desk that had belonged to her grandmother Cora, she opened the worn leather journal she had discovered in the attic. The pages were filled with her grandmother's neat, flowing script which was a window into thoughts and secrets long past.

The light from the desk lamp cast shadows across the page. Emily turned the journal to the entries around the dates of previous Lunar Blossom Festivals. Her fingers traced the lines, seeking any clue that might explain Liam's behavior, his sudden distance, and his cryptic words.

June 21, 1961, Tonight, the garden revealed its true magic under the supermoon's light. It was as if the very air shimmered with energy, a visible hum that I could almost hear. And there, at the heart of it all, stood the Guardian. His presence was both startling and comforting. He has watched over this place longer than I can remember, a protector of the celestial balance.

Emily paused, her heart skipping a beat. The Guardian—this had to be someone significant in the garden's history. But who could her grandmother have known that fit this description? And how could this person have maintained such a role for so long?

She read entries weaving tales of the garden's extraordinary occurrences and the Guardian's role in them. Cora wrote about how the Guardian was bound to the garden, a steward of its ancient magic, and how he appeared only during celestial events that aligned with the garden's deeper energies.

The Guardian does not speak much of himself, but his actions are those of someone who cares deeply for this place. He maintains the balance, ensuring that the energies do not overwhelm the space and that the cycle of life here continues as destined.

The more she read, the more she understood the weight of secrecy and responsibility that seemed to surround the Guardian. It wasn't just the garden he was protecting. It was the entire legacy of celestial phenomena that occurred here.

With each page, there was a growing respect for this mysterious Guardian and a profound sadness. He had been alone in this duty for who knew how long, watching over the garden, likely with no one truly understanding his role or the sacrifices he made. And to think that Emily had almost let the garden die.

The clock chimed softly in the background, marking the late hour. Emily closed the journal, her mind filled with new insights and emotions. She couldn't help but wonder who the Guardian was. Was he someone still connected to the garden today? Or had his identity and purpose been lost in time?

Determined, she stood up, stretching the stiffness from her limbs. She knew what she had to do. The upcoming Lunar Blossom Festival wasn't just an opportunity for her to witness the garden's magic. It was a chance to show the Guardian that they weren't alone in their efforts to protect the garden's secrets and maintain its balance.

The night was quiet as she looked out the kitchen window; the garden bathed in moonlight, serene yet alive with hidden wonders. Tomorrow, she would seek to uncover more about the Guardian and his connection to the garden. She would prepare for the festival with her friends, not just as a landowner, but as a custodian of this legacy. She turned back to the journal.

July 22, 1982

The supermoon rose tonight, and with it came the Guardian, his presence more profound than ever. He moved like a whisper, leaving trails of luminescent energy in his wake. The flowers seemed to respond to his touch, blooming brighter and standing taller. It's clear that his bond with the garden is more than just protective—it's symbiotic.

Emily's breath caught as she read the description. The Guardian's connection to the garden was indeed special, but the detail about his movements and the garden's response seemed eerily familiar.

She closed the journal, realizing her grandmother had passed before the festival in 2003, which meant there was no one to record the event. She would have to be the one to make sure there was an accounting for this festival. Her mind was buzzing with thoughts. She sensed the Guardian was closer than she realized, perhaps even someone she already knew.

The stage was set, not just for a night of wonder, but for a new beginning—for the garden and all who cherished it. The garden waited in hushed eagerness, and so did Emily, her heart full of hope and her spirit attuned to the unfolding mysteries of the celestial night that awaited them. The flowers seemed to glow a little brighter, the air buzzing with a magical energy that promised to reveal the garden's deepest secrets.

39

THE CELESTIAL CLASH

Emily was deep in sleep when a distant rumbling jarred her awake. She lay still for a moment, her heart pounding as she strained to listen. The house was quiet, but outside, something was happening. A low, eerie hum resonated through the walls, accompanied by flashes of light that seeped around the edges of the curtains.

She slipped out of bed, her bare feet silent on the wooden floor. She pulled on a robe and cautiously made her way downstairs, each step echoing in the night's stillness. Reaching the door to the garden, she hesitated with her hand on the handle before she steeled herself and opened it.

The sight that greeted her was unlike anything she had ever seen. The garden was bathed in an otherworldly glow, lights flashing erratically like an electrical storm. Pulses of energy crackled through the air, illuminating the scene in stark, surreal colors. Her eyes followed the source of the disturbance to the enchanted stream, where two figures stood locked in a fierce confrontation.

Liam and Oliver faced each other, their forms radiating contrasting energies. Liam's presence was surrounded by a soft, golden light, his hands outstretched as he channeled the spring's pure, life-giving energy. Opposite him, Oliver was a dark silhouette, shadows swirling around him like living entities, his eyes burning with spiteful determination.

"Liam!" Emily called out, her voice trembling with fear and disbelief. Both men turned toward her, and for a moment, the chaos seemed to pause.

"Emily, stay back!" Liam shouted, his voice strained as he struggled to maintain his focus against Oliver's dark energy.

Oliver sneered, his gaze flickering between Liam and Emily. "This doesn't concern you, Emily. Leave now before you get hurt."

Emily took a step forward, her determination outweighing her fear. "I won't let you destroy what my grandmother worked so hard to protect. This garden, this stream—they mean everything to this community."

Oliver's laugh was cold and mirthless. "You don't know the power that lies here. This stream is more than just water. It's a source of immense energy, and I intend to harness it."

Liam's light flared brighter, pushing back against the encroaching darkness. "Emily, the spring is the heart of the garden. If Oliver corrupts it, everything will wither and die. We must protect it."

Her mind raced. She remembered the enchanted seeds the old woman at the market had given her. Without a second thought, she ran back into the house and grabbed the small pouch from her desk drawer. Returning to the garden, she hurried to the stream, her heart pounding with urgency.

"Use these, Liam!" she cried, tossing the pouch to him. He caught it and nodded, understanding immediately.

Liam scattered the seeds into the stream. They glowed as they touched the surface, sending ripples of light through the water. The stream responded, its energy intensifying and flowing into Liam. His aura expanded, the golden light becoming a shield that pushed Oliver's shadows back.

Oliver hissed in frustration, his shadows recoiling from the pure energy. "This isn't over," he growled, his form flickering as he struggled to maintain his hold.

Liam stepped forward. His voice resonated with authority. "Leave this place, Oliver. You will not corrupt this stream. Not while I'm here."

With a final snarl, Oliver's form dissipated, the shadows melting into the night. The garden fell silent, the eerie hum fading away, leaving only the soft glow of the enchanted stream.

Emily rushed to Liam's side, her breath coming in quick gasps. "Are you alright?"

He smiled, though he looked exhausted. "I'm fine, thanks to you. Those seeds...they saved us."

She looked at the gentle, reassuring light of the stream. "What exactly happened here?"

His expression grew serious. "The stream is more than just water. It's connected to a powerful source—ancient magic tied to the very essence of life and nature. It's my duty to protect it from beings like Oliver, who seek to corrupt it."

Emily nodded, finally understanding the full scope of the battle she had stumbled upon. "We need to make sure he never comes back."

Liam looked at her, his eyes filled with determination. "We will. We'll protect this garden and the spring. For your grandmother, and for the community."

Dawn broke as Emily and Liam stood together by the stream, the light of a new day promising hope and renewal. They knew the battle wasn't over, but united in their purpose, they were stronger than ever.

"Now that things are calm again, can you explain to me more about the history between you and Oliver?" she asked.

Liam turned to her, his face shadowed. "Long ago, there was a place called Elaria, a grove of immense beauty and power. Celestial beings called Keepers, who were tasked with maintaining the balance of nature, tended it. I was one of them. So was Oliver, though he was known as Valen then."

Emily listened, her heart heavy with the weight of the revealed history.

"Valen was once a protector, like me. But he became obsessed with the power of the grove. He wanted to use its energy to dominate, to control. When he was cast out, his heart twisted with darkness and vengeance. Now, he seeks to corrupt this spring—the last remnant of Elaria's magic."

Emily's gaze shifted to the stream, understanding dawning. "How can we stop him?"

"By keeping the spring pure," Liam said. "Those seeds you brought were a powerful defense. We need to remain vigilant, Emily. Oliver won't give up easily."

The resolve in Liam's eyes mirrored what was in her own heart. "We'll do whatever it takes. For the garden, for the spring, and for everyone who believes in this place."

The battle for the spring was just beginning, but with Liam by her side, she was ready to face whatever challenges lay ahead.

Emily turned to him, a new worry line etching on her forehead. "With everything that's happened, do you think the Lunar Blossom Festival will happen?"

Liam's eyes brightened at the mention of the festival. "The Lunar Blossom Festival is a time when the garden's true magic is revealed. It's more important now than ever. It will bring the community together and strengthen the bond we need to protect this place. The stronger the bonds, the more power the spring has."

They stood by the tranquil stream, bathed in the soft light of dawn. A renewed sense of purpose engulfed them. The challenges ahead were daunting, but together, they would honor the traditions of the past and forge a future filled with light and life.

40

THE MYSTICAL GLOW

Emily's hands glided over the leaves and petals, life pulsing beneath her fingertips. The sun hung low in the sky, making the garden glow with an almost magical hue. To prepare for the Lunar Blossom Festival, she had set up lanterns that now hung from the branches, their soft light promising to illuminate the night with a gentle, mystical glow.

After the excitement with Oliver and Liam the evening before, she was exhausted but excited. Mark had returned from the city earlier that afternoon, his presence bringing a renewed sense of support. She wanted to share with him everything that had happened. It would have to wait until after the Lunar Blossom Festival. It was where her attention was focused. As they moved through the garden, they talked about her grandmother's journals, deepening their understanding of the festival's significance.

"Are you sure we have enough blankets?" Mark asked, adjusting one lantern.

"I think so," Emily replied, a smile playing on her lips. "But you know, better to have too many than not enough."

Mark chuckled, pulling her into a quick embrace. "You're right, as always."

Their conversation turned serious as they walked back toward the farmhouse. Emily glanced at Mark; her heart was heavy with thoughts she had been avoiding.

"Mark, we need to talk," she whispered.

He looked at her, concern etching his features. "What's on your mind?"

"It's about our future," Emily began, taking a deep breath. "About having children."

His expression softened, and he reached for her hand. "Emily, we've talked about this. We'll figure it out together. We love each other and we'll work it out."

"I know," she said, squeezing his hand. "But I've been thinking a lot about it lately. Watching you with Ethan...I know how much you want to be a father. And I'm scared, Mark. I'm scared that I can't give you that."

He stopped walking and turned to face her, his eyes filled with love and determination. "Emily, we've faced so many challenges together. This is just another one. Whether we have children of our own or we adopt, it doesn't matter. What matters is that we face it together."

A weight lifted off her shoulders, and she nodded, tears brimming in her eyes. "You're right. I'm just so afraid of the strain it might put on us like before. I love you."

"We'll handle it. One step at a time," Mark said, pulling her into a comforting hug. "I love you, too."

They held each other. A renewed sense of hope filled them. They could face whatever the future held.

"Everything looks wonderful." Maggie said, walking toward Emily to hug her. "I can't wait for tonight."

"Thanks, Maggie," Emily replied.

The rest of their friends joined them in the garden. Maya and Alex were admiring the preparations and chatting excitedly as they showed off Ethan to everyone. Liam was present too, though his eyes often wandered to the edges of the garden where the shadows were deepening.

"Liam, are you alright? You seem a bit...distracted. You have me worried after last night."

He turned to her, a gentle smile masking the complexity of his thoughts. "I'm fine, Emily. Just thinking about some personal matters."

"It's not Oliver again, is it?"

"No." Liam shook his head, a slight smile escaping his lips. "He's gone for now."

Emily studied his face, sensing there was more he wasn't saying, but she didn't press him. "Well, if you need to talk, I'm here," she offered.

Liam nodded. "Thank you. I appreciate your concern. It means a lot."

The evening progressed, and strange, magical occurrences intensified in the garden. Flowers that only bloomed under moonlight opened, their petals shimmering with an ethereal light. A magical hum floated in the air, and everyone could feel the energy coursing through the garden.

There was a mix of excitement and apprehension. The night was finally here, the Lunar Blossom Festival that her grandmother had written about in her journals. She glanced around at her friends, sensing a deep connection and gratitude. They were all here, ready to experience the garden's magic together.

Mark squeezed her hand, bringing her back to the present. "You ready for this?" he asked, his eyes shining with excitement.

"I am," Emily replied, her voice filled with wonder. "I really am."

The sun dipped below the horizon, and the first stars appeared in the sky. The garden transformed. Lanterns cast a soft, warm glow, and the flowers seemed to dance in the gentle breeze. They were ready for a night of wonder, a gathering that would bridge the past with the present and, perhaps, open the door to new beginnings.

The feeling of anticipation and magic was tangible. A profound connection to her grandmother's legacy and a renewed sense of purpose distracted her. She glanced at Liam, who stood at the edge of the garden, his face lit by the soft glow of the lanterns. There was something about him, something she couldn't quite put her finger on. After last night, she'd learned not to be surprised by anything he did.

The night deepened, and Emily's thoughts turned to the mysteries that awaited them. The garden was alive with secrets, and she was ready to uncover them. With her friends by her side, there was a sense of hope and excitement for the future.

The garden waited in muted excitement, and so did Emily, her heart full of hope and her spirit attuned to the unfolding mysteries of the celestial night that awaited them. The flowers glowed faintly in the twilight as if sharing her excitement, and the whispers of the past seemed to grow louder, promising secrets and magic yet to be revealed.

41

THE LUNAR BLOSSOM FESTIVAL

The moon began its ascent into the night sky. The garden buzzed with a palpable sense of anticipation. Emily, Mark, Maggie, Maya, Alex, Ethan, and the rest of the community gathered among the flowers and lanterns, their faces illuminated by the soft, magical glow of the garden. The supermoon, a brilliant orb of silvery light, cast its ethereal glow over everything, making the garden seem otherworldly.

Emily took a deep breath, the garden's energy coursing through her. She glanced at Mark, who stood beside her, his hand cradling hers. "Are you ready?" she whispered, her voice tinged with excitement.

Mark nodded, his eyes shining with wonder. "I've never been more ready."

The crowd settled onto the blankets and cushions spread around the garden. Their eyes turned toward the sky as the supermoon reached its zenith. The garden responded to the celestial event with a breathtaking display of magic. Flowers that had been tightly closed during the day unfurled their petals in synchronized harmony, revealing colors and patterns and iridescent hues that seemed alive with motion. A soft, resonant hum filled the air, an otherworldly melody echoing from the earth's depths.

Emily's eyes drifted to Liam, who stood apart from the gathering. His eyes were closed, his face calm yet focused. Around him, a shimmering aura took shape, shifting like liquid silver under the moonlight. The energy coalesced, growing brighter and more defined with every heartbeat. Emily's chest tightened, a deep knowing settling within her. Something extraordinary was about to unfold.

Suddenly, the Guardian spirit appeared just as her grandmother had described. Its form was breathtaking—a luminous being of pure light and serenity, standing at the boundary between human and celestial. Its shape was humanoid, yet ethereal, with flowing, translucent robes that shimmered with the colors of the rainbow—soft blues, silvers, and purples. Trails of sparkling stardust followed its every movement, falling gently onto the petals below and causing the garden to shimmer with renewed vitality. Its face was indistinct yet conveyed a profound sense of peace and timeless wisdom. Eyes like glowing constellations scanned the crowd with a gaze that seemed to see through to their souls.

The Guardian moved gracefully among the blooms, its presence sending ripples of luminescent energy through the garden. Wherever it passed, flowers bloomed brighter, their colors deepening and their petals trembling with a subtle life of their own. The air vibrated with a harmonic resonance that seemed to connect the heavens, the earth, and the gathered community.

Emily's breath caught as the Guardian's radiant form turned toward Liam. The shimmering aura surrounding him intensified, enveloping him in a cocoon of light. The gathered crowd gasped in awe, their wonder a palpable thread uniting them in the moment.

Liam's form began to shift and change, his features softening and elongating into something familiar yet unearthly. His body radiated the same celestial glow as the Guardian, and his outline blurred as though he were dissolving into the moonlit ether. As the transformation completed, Emily felt a rush of clarity.

Liam was the Guardian—the protector of the garden's celestial magic, its eternal steward. His presence here was no accident. He had been chosen to uphold the delicate balance between earth and sky, nurturing the garden's magical legacy for generations to come.

The community watched in reverent silence as the newly revealed Guardian stood among them, embodying hope, harmony, and the enduring connection between humanity and the natural world.

Liam's eyes glowed with a deep, ancient wisdom. Now the Guardian, he looked around at the gathered community, his expression one of serenity and purpose.

"Friends," he began, his voice resonating with a soothing, powerful tone. "I have been entrusted with protecting this garden and its celestial magic. For generations, the Guardian has ensured that the balance of nature and the garden's energies are maintained."

He paused, his gaze sweeping over the captivated faces before him. "The Lunar Blossom Festival is a time of renewal and healing, when the garden's deepest secrets are revealed. This night, you are all witnesses to the magic that binds us to this land and to each other."

Respect and admiration surged through Emily. His role as the Guardian was a heavy responsibility, one that he shouldered with quiet strength and dedication. She stepped forward, her voice filled with wonder. "Liam, I understand now. Of course, a Keeper would also be the Guardian."

He smiled gently, the surrounding light flickering softly. "The Guardian's role is not one of glory or recognition. It is a sacred duty to protect and nurture the garden's magic. I had to ensure that the knowledge and power remained safe until the right time came for it to be shared."

Maggie, Maya, and Alex exchanged awed glances, their initial shock giving way to understanding and respect. The community, too, grasped the significance of Liam's revelation.

Liam continued, "Tonight, under the light of the supermoon, we are all part of this magic. The garden's energy flows through each of us, connecting us to the past, present, and future. As we move forward, it is our collective duty to protect and cherish this sacred place."

He moved among the crowd, his presence a comforting reminder of the garden's timeless magic. The flowers glowed with an otherworldly light, their petals seeming to whisper to those who listened closely.

Emily stepped closer, her heart swelling with gratitude and a sense of destiny fulfilled. "Thank you, Liam. For everything."

He nodded, his eyes meeting hers with a deep, knowing gaze. "Thank you, Emily. Your grandmother would be proud of you. Now that you know all the garden's secrets, it's up to you to pass them along. To provide another protector for the garden like your grandmother provided you. Together, we will continue to honor her legacy and the magic of this place."

The night continued with a sense of unity and purpose. The community gathered around him, sharing stories and dreams under the light of the supermoon. The garden, vibrant and alive, seemed to embrace them all, its magic weaving a tapestry of connection and renewal.

The festival drew to a close. A profound sense of peace consumed her. The garden's secrets had been revealed, and with them, a new chapter had begun. She glanced at Mark, who was smiling beside her and sensed a rush of joy and hope. Their journey was far from over, but together, with their friends and the magic of the garden, they were ready to face whatever the future held.

The soft glow of lanterns, the hum of the garden's energy, and the whispers of the past were noticeable. Emily knew that the garden's magic would continue to guide and protect them, its legacy living on in the hearts of all who cherished it.

42

A NEW BEGINNING

The morning after the Lunar Blossom Festival dawned with a soft, golden light that filtered through the leaves and petals of the garden. The scent of blooming flowers was in the air and the gentle hum of nature waking up. Emily stood at the edge of the garden, her heart still brimming with the magic of the previous night.

Now revealed as the Guardian, Liam stood beside her, his presence radiating a quiet strength. His transformation had not only changed his appearance but also deepened the bond he shared with the garden and its celestial magic.

Emily turned to him, her eyes filled with curiosity and admiration. "I can't believe you've been the Guardian all this time. Why didn't you tell us?"

He smiled, his gaze steady and calm. "The role of the Guardian is to protect the garden's magic and ensure its balance. It's a responsibility that requires secrecy to maintain the delicate equilibrium. But now that you know, we can work together to safeguard this place."

Emily nodded, understanding the weight of his duty. "I'm honored to be a part of this. Together, we'll continue to honor my grandmother's legacy."

They walked through the garden. The flowers seemed to lean toward Liam, recognizing their protector. A deep sense of peace appeared, knowing that the garden was in safe hands.

Later that morning, Emily gathered with Mark, Maggie, Maya, and Alex in the farmhouse kitchen. Ethan was asleep in Maya's arms. The atmosphere contained a renewed sense of purpose and excitement for the future.

"I still can't believe it," Maggie said, her eyes wide with wonder. "Liam, the Guardian of the garden. It's like something out of a fairy tale."

"It really is," Alex agreed. "But it makes perfect sense. The way the garden responds to him, it's like they're connected on a deeper level."

Maya nodded. "We're all connected to this place. And now, more than ever, we need to protect and cherish it."

A wave of nausea washed over Emily. She excused herself and went to the bathroom, suddenly lightheaded. After a few moments, the nausea passed, but a lingering sense of unease remained. She was sure it was just the excitement of the previous nights, but she made an appointment with her doctor, just to be sure.

A few days later, Mark was preparing to return to the city as she sat in the doctor's office, nervously tapping her foot. When the doctor entered with a warm smile, her heart raced.

"Emily, we've gone through all the results of your blood tests," the doctor said, her eyes shining with joy. "You're pregnant."

Emily's breath caught in her throat, tears welling up in her eyes as she remembered what Liam had said about the night of the Lunar Blossom Festival. That it was up to her to pass along the garden's secrets. To provide another protector like her grandmother had provided Emily. That they would honor the garden's magic and her grandmother's legacy together.

"I'm...I'm pregnant?"

"Yes," the doctor said gently. "We'll want you to make another appointment for a few weeks from now, but as of now, everything looks good."

"Of course." Emily raised her hands to her mouth. She wanted to scream with excitement.

Leaving the doctor's office, her mind was a whirlwind of emotions. She had given up hope of ever becoming pregnant, and now, this unexpected miracle filled her with a joy she could hardly contain.

When she arrived back at the farmhouse, she was hoping Mark hadn't left yet. He was waiting for her, his expression filled with concern. "Emily, are you okay? I decided not to leave until you returned. I wanted to make sure everything was alright. I should have gone with you."

She nodded, tears streaming down her face. "Mark, I'm pregnant."

His eyes widened with shock and then filled with joy. He pulled her into a tight embrace, his voice choked with emotion. "Pregnant? That's incredible. We're going to be parents."

"It must have been the magic of the garden. I'm so happy."

They held each other. A profound sense of gratitude for the garden's magic and the unexpected blessings it had brought into their lives washed through her.

The news of Emily's pregnancy quickly spread through the community, filling everyone with joy and hope. Liam, in his role as the Guardian, gathered the community in the garden to share their future plans.

"Friends, the garden's magic has blessed us in many ways," Liam began, his voice resonating with authority and warmth. "We must continue to protect and cherish this place, ensuring that its magic endures for future generations."

Emily stepped forward, her hand resting on her stomach. "This garden has given us so much. It's a place of healing, hope, and renewal. Together, we'll honor its magic and ensure that its legacy lives on."

The community cheered, their voices filled with determination and unity. They discussed plans for educational programs and initiatives to preserve the garden's magic, ensuring that the knowledge and wisdom of the past would be passed down to future generations.

The days turned into weeks. The garden flourished under the care and dedication of the community. Emily and Mark prepared for the arrival of their child, their hearts filled with love and anticipation.

One evening, as the sun set over the garden, Emily and Liam walked among the flowers, their conversation turning to the future.

"What will happen now that we know about your role as the Guardian?" Emily asked, her voice thoughtful.

"We will continue to protect the garden's magic together," Liam replied. "The knowledge and responsibilities will be shared, ensuring that the garden remains a place of wonder and healing."

Emily nodded, recognizing a deep sense of purpose. "Thank you, Liam. For everything."

The stars twinkled in the night sky. A connection to the garden and the community filled her. The magic of the Lunar Blossom Festival had not only revealed the garden's secrets but also brought them closer together, forging bonds that would last a lifetime.

The garden waited in quiet longing, its magic a constant presence that guided and protected them. Emily knew they were united in their love for the garden and each other.

With Liam's guidance and the support of their friends, Emily and Mark looked forward to a future filled with hope, magic, and the promise of new beginnings. The garden's legacy would live on, cherished and protected by all who called it home.

The garden glowed softly under the light of the moon. A testament to the enduring power of nature and the magic that connected them all. There was a sense of peace, knowing that love and the timeless magic of the garden surrounded her.

43

ROSIE'S REVELATION

Emily was more connected to the garden's magic than ever before; her role as its protector now intertwined with her own journey toward motherhood. The garden had become a place of beauty and a living, breathing part of her family's legacy.

One evening, after a long day of planning with the community, Emily found herself alone in her bedroom. Mark had traveled to the city on business. The house was quiet, and the gentle hum of life around her provided a soothing backdrop as she prepared for bed. She placed her hand on her growing belly, smiling at the thought of the child growing inside her. The future felt full of promise.

As she drifted off to sleep, the comforting presence of the garden seemed to follow her into her dreams. Emily found herself in the garden, but it was more vivid and alive than she had ever seen it. The colors were richer, the scents were intoxicating, and a soft, magical glow was in the air.

She walked through the garden, an overwhelming sense of peace washing over her. As she approached the ancient oak tree, she noticed something unusual—a tiny figure sitting at the base of the tree, bathed in the golden light that seemed to emanate from the earth itself.

It was Rosie. In this dream, Rosie wasn't just a simple doll. She was alive, her fabric eyes sparkling with warmth and wisdom.

She knelt beside Rosie, wonder and familiarity washing over her. "Rosie," Emily whispered, her voice filled with awe, "is this real?"

Rosie looked up at Emily, her expression tender and knowing. "It is as real as it needs to be," she replied, her voice full of wisdom. "I've been with you for so long, watching over you, protecting you, just as your grandmother wished."

Tears welled up in Emily's eyes. "You've been there for me through everything, haven't you? Even when I didn't realize it?"

Rosie nodded, her small hand reaching out to gently touch Emily's. "Yes, my dear. I have kept your dreams safe, guided you through your darkest nights, and now, as you prepare to bring new life into this world, it's time for me to pass on my protection to your daughter."

"My daughter?" Emily smiled as she ran her hand over her belly.

Rosie smiled, her glow intensifying slightly. "Yes, Emily. The love and magic surrounding you will now be passed on to your daughter. She will be born into a world where the garden's magic and your love will guide her, just as they have guided you."

Emily's heart filled with gratitude. "Thank you, Rosie. For everything."

Rosie's light seemed to pulse with affection. "You are strong, Emily. Stronger than you know. And your daughter will be strong too. But she will also need your guidance, your love, and the magic of this place. I will be with her just as I have been with you."

As Emily listened to Rosie's words, the surrounding garden glowed brighter, the magic of the place wrapping around her like a warm embrace. Deep in her heart, she knew that Rosie's journey with her was coming to a close, but that the doll's protection would continue with her daughter.

The dream faded, the vibrant colors and soft light blending into the warm darkness of sleep. Emily felt herself being gently pulled back to the waking world, but not before Rosie's last words echoed in her mind.

"Remember, Emily, the magic of this garden lives on in you, in your family, and now, in your daughter. Keep it safe, and it will always protect you."

Emily woke with the first light of dawn filtering through her windows. The dream lingered in her mind, so vivid and real that she could still sense Rosie's warmth. She turned her head to see Rosie in her place on the pillow, looking just as she had in the dream, but now with a subtle, comforting presence that filled the room.

With a smile, she picked up Rosie and held her close, feeling the weight of the legacy she was about to pass on. "Thank you," she whispered, her voice filled with love and determination. She placed the doll gently on her growing belly, knowing that Rosie's protection would now extend to her daughter.

The dream gave Emily the clarity and comfort she needed. She knew that when the time was right, she would pass Rosie on to her daughter, continuing the circle of love, protection, and magic that had been passed down through the generations to her.

44

THE GUARDIAN'S EMBRACE

The community of Blue Ridge Haven came together to celebrate their unique heritage and the magic of the garden, more united than ever after the Lunar Blossom Festival.

The sun rose on another beautiful morning. Emily sat in the garden, reflecting on the journey that had brought her here. She sensed her grandmother's presence in every leaf and petal, knowing that Cora would be proud of her for embracing the garden's magic and her role as its protector. The vibrant blooms seemed to sing with the joy of new beginnings.

The gentle rustling of leaves interrupted Emily's thoughts. She turned to see Liam approaching, his presence now more ethereal yet grounded in the earth he had sworn to protect.

"Good morning, Liam," Emily greeted him with a warm smile.

"Good morning, Emily," he replied, his voice carrying the serenity of the garden. "How are you feeling?"

She placed a hand on her growing belly, her eyes shining with happiness. "I'm wonderful. This place...it's given me so much hope."

Liam nodded, his gaze thoughtful. "The garden's magic is a gift, one that we must continue to nurture and protect. There's something I want to show you."

Curious, she followed him to a secluded part of the garden, where an ancient willow tree stood, its branches swaying gently in the breeze. At its base, flowers of every color bloomed, their petals glistening with dew that sparkled like diamonds in the morning light.

"This willow has always been a focal point of the garden's magic," Liam explained. "It's where the energies of the earth and the celestial align. Your grandmother knew this and often meditated here to connect with the garden's deeper essence."

Emily knelt beside the willow, sensing the powerful energy that radiated from the earth. "It's incredible, Liam. I can sense the connection, the harmony."

Liam placed a hand on the tree, closing his eyes. "As the Guardian, it's my duty to maintain this balance. But the garden's magic thrives on community and shared responsibility. You and your friends are now its caretakers, its protectors."

Emily stood, recognizing the weight of her new role and the strength that came from knowing she was not alone. "We'll honor this place, Liam. We'll ensure that its magic endures."

They walked back to the main part of the garden, where they were joined by Mark, Maggie, Maya, Alex, Ethan, and other members of the community. Everyone gathered around, their faces alight with hope and determination.

Liam addressed them, his voice resonating with authority and warmth. "The garden's magic is a shared gift, one that connects us to the past, the present, and the future. We must protect and cherish it, ensuring that its legacy lives on."

Maggie stepped forward, her eyes bright with enthusiasm. "We've been discussing educational programs and initiatives to preserve the garden's magic. We want to teach future generations about its importance."

Alex nodded in agreement. "And we can document the garden's history and the Lunar Blossom Festivals so that the knowledge is never lost."

A surge of pride and gratitude for her friends and the community rushed through her. "Together, we'll create something beautiful, something lasting. The garden's magic will continue to thrive."

The community discussed their plans. There was a gentle tug on Emily's heart. She turned to Mark, who smiled at her, his eyes filled with love and excitement for the future.

Later that evening, as the sun dipped below the horizon, Emily and Mark stood at the edge of the garden, watching as the first stars appeared in the sky. The soft glow of lanterns illuminated the flowers, creating a scene of tranquil beauty.

Mark wrapped an arm around Emily, his hand resting on her belly. "I can't believe how much has changed," he whispered. "We have a child on the way, and this garden...it's a part of our family."

She leaned into him; her heart was full of love. "It is a part of our family. This garden has brought us together in ways I never imagined."

They stood there, wrapped in each other's arms. A sense of peace and fulfillment showed itself. The garden's magic had not only revealed its secrets but also brought healing and hope to their lives.

The willow sways gently in the evening breeze, its branches whispering secrets of the past and promises of the future.

45

THE FINALE

The garden was alive with the hum of life as Blue Ridge Haven gathered to celebrate its restoration. Soft lanterns glowed like fireflies, strung between the branches of the ancient oak and the gazebo that now stood proudly at the garden's heart. Flowers bloomed in vibrant harmony. Their colors illuminated by the golden light of the setting sun.

Neighbors mingled along the winding paths, their voices mingling with the soft music carried on the breeze. A small group of children giggled as they chased glowing fairies flitting between the blossoms.

Maya sat beneath the ancient willow, cradling her infant son, Ethan, in her arms. The baby gurgled happily, waving his tiny fists in the air as if trying to grasp the glowing lights hovering just out of reach. "Do you see the fairies, little one?" Maya cooed, her face glowing with maternal joy. "They're here to celebrate with us."

Emily stood at the edge of the gathering. Her hands nervously clasped together as she took in the scene. Maggie approached, her silver hair shimmering in the evening light, carrying a tray of refreshments. "Why so quiet, dear? This is your moment."

Smiling, Emily's heart swelled with gratitude as she watched the community enjoying the space that had become her sanctuary. "I'm just taking it all in. It feels... surreal."

Maggie nodded knowingly. "Cora would be proud. She always believed this garden was meant to be shared. And now, thanks to you, it is."

Her attention shifting to Maya, Emily watched as she rocked Ethan gently, humming a soft tune. The sight warmed Emily's heart, reminding her of the garden's promise of renewal and growth.

A hand touched Emily's shoulder. She turned to see Liam, his presence steady and reassuring as always. "They're waiting for you," he said with a small smile, gesturing toward a makeshift stage adorned with flowers.

Taking a deep breath, Emily made her way to the platform, her steps sure but her heart racing. Mark stood near the front of the crowd, his supportive smile anchoring her as she faced the gathered friends, neighbors, and family.

"Thank you all for being here tonight," she began, her voice carrying over the quiet murmur of the crowd. "This garden isn't just about flowers or trees. It's about community, healing, and second chances. It's about remembering where we come from and finding hope for where we're going. My grandmother believed in this garden's magic, and thanks to all of you, it's alive again. Stronger than ever."

She gestured toward the vibrant expanse of plants and pathways behind her. "This place is a testament to what we can accomplish together. And as we move forward, I hope this garden will continue to grow. Not just with flowers, but with stories, friendships, and the kind of love that makes anything possible."

The crowd erupted into applause, the sound carrying into the twilight.

As the evening deepened, music filled the air, and lanterns were released into the sky, their gentle glow blending with the stars. Emily wandered through the garden, pausing to capture moments with her camera: Alex showing a group of teens how to build planter boxes;

Maggie laughing with Liam over a shared joke; and Maya, sitting beneath the willow, holding Ethan close as he drifted off to sleep.

Finally, Emily gathered her closest friends and neighbors near the ancient willow tree for a photograph. Maya carefully brought Ethan over, nestling him into her arms as she joined the group.

Mark stood by Emily's side, his arm wrapped protectively around her, and Maggie, Liam, Alex, and Maya crowded in close. Ethan yawned, his tiny hand clutching Maya's finger as the camera's shutter clicked, capturing not just a moment but the heart of their journey.

Emily glanced at the image on her camera's screen. The faces of her friends, her family, and her community glowed with hope and unity, framed by the vibrant blooms of the garden. Her heart swelled with peace. The garden had given her more than she could have imagined—more than she even dared to hope.

As she slipped her camera into its case, Emily turned toward the ancient willow. Its branches swayed gently in the evening breeze, as if in silent approval. "Thank you, Grandma," she whispered, feeling her grandmother's presence as a comforting warmth in her chest.

The stars blinked into view one by one, casting their light over the garden and its gathered caretakers. Emily took Mark's hand, their fingers entwining as they walked toward the house. Behind them, the garden glowed softly in the twilight, a promise of growth, love, and enduring magic.

EPILOGUE

Four years had passed since the fateful night of the Lunar Blossom Festival 2024, and Blue Ridge Haven had flourished under the careful stewardship of its devoted community. The garden, vibrant and lush, continued to be the heart and soul of the town, its magic a cherished secret shared by all who lived there.

Emily walked through the garden with a small child's hand tucked into hers. Her daughter, Cora, was a curious and lively spirit, her bright eyes taking in every wonder the garden offered. Rosie was safe in Cora's embrace. Mark followed close behind. Their son, Max, perched happily on his shoulders, giggling as he pointed at the colorful flowers.

The garden had become a living classroom for Cora and Max, where they learned about the magic of nature, the importance of balance, and the legacy of their great-grandmother, Cora. As Emily watched her children explore the garden, a single flower bloomed unexpectedly at their feet. She often sensed her presence in the garden, guiding her, just as she guided her children. The wind would carry the faint sound of her grandmother's laughter.

Liam, still the Guardian, watched over the garden with the same dedication and serenity. He had become a beloved figure in the community, his role now openly acknowledged and respected. His bond with the garden was as strong as ever, and he shared his knowledge freely, ensuring that the garden's magic would never be forgotten.

The community had grown, and with it, their commitment to preserving the garden's magic. Educational programs flourished, teaching both young and old about the garden's history and its celestial wonders. Festivals and celebrations were held regularly, bringing everyone together to honor the garden and its guardian.

On evenings of full moons, as the sun set in a blaze of orange and gold, the community gathered. Lanterns hung from the trees, casting a warm glow over the assembled crowd. Emily stood at the center, holding Cora's hand while Mark held Max. Liam stood beside them, a proud and serene presence.

"Tonight," Emily began, her voice carrying through the quiet garden, "we gather to celebrate not just the magic of this place but the legacy of love and care that has brought us here. This garden is a testament to the power of community and the enduring spirit of those who came before us."

Liam stepped forward, his eyes glowing with an inner light. "The garden's magic is a gift, one that we must continue to nurture and protect. It connects us to the past, grounds us in the present, and guides us into the future. Together, we ensure that this sacred place remains a source of wonder and healing for generations to come."

Emily sensed deep fulfillment as the ceremony continued. She looked at her children, knowing they would grow up with the same love and respect for the garden she inherited from her grandmother. The garden's magic would continue to thrive, a living legacy that bound them all together.

The first stars appeared in the sky as the night grew darker, and the garden glowed with a soft, ethereal light. The flowers shimmered, their petals whispering secrets of the past and promises of the future. The community stood in awe, united in their love for the garden and the magic that connected them all.

Emily looked at Mark, who smiled at her, his eyes filled with love and pride. Together, they had faced challenges and embraced new beginnings. The garden had been a guiding light, its magic a constant presence that had brought them closer together.

Standing tall and wise, the ancient willow tree seemed to watch over them, its branches swaying gently in the breeze. There was a profound sense of peace, knowing that the garden's legacy was in safe hands. With Liam as the Guardian and the community's unwavering dedication, the garden would continue to thrive, a beacon of hope and magic for all who sought its solace.

The garden waited in barely contained excitement, its magic a timeless presence that guided and protected them. Emily knew they were ready to face whatever the future held, united in their love for the garden and each other. Magic would continue to flourish, a testament to the enduring power of nature and the bonds that connected them all.

With the stars twinkling above and the garden glowing softly below, fulfillment and hope appeared to Emily. The journey had brought them to this moment, and she knew that the garden's magic would continue to guide them, lighting their way into a future filled with wonder and new beginnings. She had marked November 20, 2045, on her calendar as the date of the next Lunar Blossom Festival.

ABOUT THE AUTHOR

C. Deanne Rowe was born and raised in southwest Oklahoma. She has also lived in Nebraska, Texas, and California. Iowa has been her home for over thirty years where she lives with her husband, two children and their spouses, five grandchildren, the memory of her hero teacup toy poodle, Allie, and her new rescue French Bulldog, Kendell.

She has always loved writing poetry and short stories and became a published romance author later in life. She has published thirteen books of her own, three in her Valley Series, six in her Cowboy Temptation Series, three in her Puckerbrush series and one non-fiction, Comforted From Heaven. As one of the Stiletto Girls, she is an author of eleven novellas in the Stiletto Girls Series.

Learn more about C. Deanne Rowe, her books, sign up for her newsletter, and receive a free ebook at:

www.cdeannerowe.com

ALSO BY C. DEANNE ROWE

Valley Series:

In The Heart of Valley

Return to Valley

Dream of Valley

Puckerbrush Series:

Secrets of Puckerbrush

Return to Puckerbrush

Beyond Puckerbrush

Cowboy Temptation Series:

Colt and Cassy

Southern Sophistication

Cowboy Owns Her Heart

Accidental Cowgirl

Alana's List

Remember Me

Miller Canyon Ranch Series

Bread, Beignets, and Cowboy Boots

The Family Tree

Through My Eyes

After A Broken Heart

Just One Kiss

Non-Fiction:

Comforted From Heaven—the true account of my near-death experience